Book II of S.O.L.A.D.™:
The Angelo™ & Angeline™ Chronicles

S.O.L.A.D.™

"It's Just the Beginning!"

by

Tyrone Tony Reed Jr.

What People Are Saying About the S.O.L.A.D.™ novel series

"BEST-SELLER, FOR SURE!"

I LOVED this book! The characters are easy to relate to, the action is suspenseful and thrilling, and the story is so captivating. I found myself recognizing my faults and excuses in the actions of the main characters. And, through their struggles and growth, I realized I could also recognize my strengths. This is one of those books that, once read, makes the reader want to change the world. If you've ever felt like things are hopeless, you need to read this book. If you've ever felt like a nothing, you need to read this book. If you've ever told yourself that God can't use you to make a difference, you need to read this book.

-Ashley Holzhausen
beta reader and editor

"BEST BOOK EVER!!!!"

This book is the best book i have ever read, it's like I am in the book! When is the sequel coming out, I would love to buy it, Tyrone Reed Jr. Is an amazing author! If he and James Patterson teamed up to write a book, it would FLY off the shelves, if I ever see him in Houston, I will ask for an autograph!

-Richard Wells

"HUNGRY FOR MORE"

From a plot and character standpoint, S.O.L.A.D.™ has done an outstanding job of keeping me engaged and wanting to see what happens next. That's the primary thing I am looking for when I read a story, and S.O.L.A.D.™ has delivered. I whipped through the book at warp speed, and when I hit the end--which was like a punch in the gut and I am sure will be especially so to those who are from Memphis or others who know just how much the city has struggled and believe in its potential to rise above its challenges--I found myself left with questions that I badly wanted to resolve. I know I can't be the only reader out there wanting to know if a certain someone is lying about a predestination paradox. What a way to bring together science fiction fun, and spiritual warfare, to leave the reader
with those sorts of questions!

-Floyd Waters

"SO GOOD!!!"

This was a great book. I can't wait for the next in the series to be published. I'm spreading the word to my family and friends to read S.O.L.A.D.™ It was so good I had to read it again.

-Renee Brown

"ENTERTAINING
AND ENLIGHTENING"

Interesting blend of superhero characters on an action-packed Pilgrim's Progress type journey in a parallel world. Made for an entertaining and enlightening read. Ready to pick up the sequel soon!

-Angie
on *Goodreads*

This book is dedicated to my dad,
Tyrone Reed Sr.

1953-2014

You asked me about this book almost daily and now
that it is complete, I pray that God gave you an
advance copy and that you love it.

I think about you every day and wish you were still
here. We miss you so much and we know that we will
see you again in Heaven.

Love you always.
Thanks for being the best dad you could be.

*This book is also dedicated to my father-in-law,
David Lee Cheshier*

1952-2014

*You unexpectedly passed from this earthly realm
seven weeks before my dad, but you are missed just the
same.*

*You showed me so much kindness, love and respect
and I will never, ever forget that.*

*Rest in Heaven knowing that your daughter is being
loved and cared for just like you would want her to be,
like the beautiful, smart queen she is.*

*To all the Soldiers of Light who asked for more
adventures of Angelo and Angeline,*

*It's because of your love and support and your weekly
and daily inquiries of what happens next in this saga
that more of these stories will continue to come and
someday soon, be seen in theaters and on televisions
around the world.*

*Continue to let me know what you enjoy about this
series, what you have questions about and what you
would like to see next.*

*And always remember, never give up on your dreams
because they can and will come true. Once your
dreams come true, please help others make their
dreams come true too.*

Table of Contents

Beginning:
The War Always, Always, Hits Home

Middle:
Trials & Tribulations

End:
Light Against Darkness

Acknowledgements

About the S.O.L.A.D. novel series

About the Author

How to Become a
Soldier of Light Against Darkness™

Beginning:
The War Always, Always, Hits Home

1

Prologue: A Year of Waiting

Two men stood near a roped off area in the middle of a dimly lit library. They anxiously waited for something to happen. There was nothing special inside the area, just a cold, barren, wood floor. Yet, the men had been waiting for over four hours for that to change at a moment's notice.

"We've been coming in here, back and forth, for over a year, waiting for that portal to open up again," the white, taller, younger man said.

"I know, Jeff, but, it's going to open any day now," the black, shorter, older man said.

"You've been saying that nearly every day since Kevin and Juanita left, Jerry," Jeffrey Wardlaw said.

"I know, but this time, we have confirmation from 'him,'" Jerry Wiseman said.

"I know, I know," Jeff said as he rummaged through one of his two duffel bags. A glowing, white, collapsible staff sat inside a medium-sized, bright orange quiver on Jeff's back. "So many things have changed in a year, especially since he arrived. Speaking of which, shouldn't we be taking him with us?"

Jerry scratched his bald head. "No. He told us that Kevin and Juanita aren't supposed to know about him or who we found in the Demon Master's castle yet."

"But, they have the right to know, J."

"I know they do and I want to tell them, but he told us that it isn't time for them to know and we promised to keep him and the discovery a secret," Jerry said. "After everything he has done since he got here, we owe him that. We would have never found her without him. Besides, he hasn't given us any reason to distrust him."

Jeff frowned. "I know, but I don't like it. And I really hate that we have to keep referring to him as 'him.'"

"I don't like it either, but he said he has to remain a secret for now," Jerry said. "We don't know if any of the Demon Master's lieutenants are still on New Earth or what they might do if they learned about him. Besides, we need to focus on the journey we are about to embark on. The portal turned red after Kevin and Juanita went through it. I believe something went into the portal behind them and I want to make sure they are okay."

A small, blue light suddenly appeared within the ropes and expanded into a large, blue, swirling portal.

"It's time," Jerry said. "Do you have enough medicine for the trip?"

Jeff grabbed his duffel bags and sat them inches away from the portal. He looked through one of the bags and pulled out a glowing, white box. "Jesheena gave me a week's supply. I just hope it's enough."

"It will be," Jerry said. "You just have to stay in control of your emotions, more specifically, your anger. God will give you the strength you need."

"I know," Jeff said. "I just have one question: how are we going to get back home?"

Jerry patted Jeff on his back as he grabbed one of the duffel bags. "Have faith and pray that Kevin, Juanita and their world are all right."

Jeff grabbed the second duffel bag and the two men entered the portal, which quickly closed behind them.

Tyrone Tony Reed Jr.

2

"...It's Just the Beginning!"

Hundreds of bolts of lightning lit up the dark, stormy skies over the city of Memphis as Angelo slammed into the belly of a giant black dragon.

"This thing doesn't want to go down," Angelo said to Angeline through his headset.

The dragon glowed bright red and exhaled red flames out of its mouth toward Angelo, who blocked the flames with his shield.

"Then we've got to make it go down," Angeline said as she held her hands out toward the dragon's mouth.

A purple force field formed around the dragon's mouth, preventing it from shooting out anymore flames.

"Thanks, Angeline," Angelo said as he plunged his sword into the dragon's back. He moved it around in a circle, yanked it out and pushed several purity bombs into the wound.

The red glow of the dragon dimmed as the dragon's body began glowing white from the inside. Beams of white light shot out from under the dragon's scales and seconds later, the dragon burst into bright, white ashes.

"One dragon down, about a thousand demons to go," Angeline said as she flew up beside Angelo.

The two heroes hovered around in the sky, avoiding lightning strikes as they surveyed the city.

"We need to find out who is doing this," Angelo said.

"Do you think...?" Angeline was afraid to finish her thought. She was afraid if she said the words "Demon

Master" aloud, she would conjure him up from the dead.

"He's dead," Angelo said, appearing to have read Angeline's mind. "There's no doubt about it. I saw him die and I made sure it was permanent."

"Well, I guess that's a relief. But, you know what they say, 'better the devil you know than the one you don't."

"Well, Angie, that devil is dead," Angelo said.

"I believe you," Angeline said before smacking Angelo in the back of his head. "And you're not nicknaming me 'Angie.'"

Angelo smirked as he looked down at the city of Memphis. He knew that brief, familiar interaction with Angeline would probably be the last one for a few hours or more.

"We're trapped in the city," Angeline said as she looked up at a faint whitish-reddish dome that encased them and the rest of the city.

"Good," Angelo said. "That means we don't have to worry about any of these demons getting out and going somewhere else."

"Always the optimistic," Angeline said.

"No, but I'm trying to be," Angelo said.

Angelo's mind flashed back to Dark Earth and the images the Demon Master threw into his mind. "I can't become him."

"Become who?" Angeline asked Angelo.

Before Angelo could answer, the heroes noticed seven red-winged, armored demon soldiers, armed with battle-axes, heading toward them.

Angelo unsheathed his Sword of Faith, but quickly realized there was no need.

The demons were unable to reach Angelo or Angeline because the demons were encased in one of Angeline's force fields.

The demons pounded on the force field as hard as they could and it didn't bother Angeline at all.

"They are really trying to get out," Angeline said as she formed a tennis ball size hole in the force field. "Your turn, Angelo."

Angelo reached into one of the pouches on his belt and pulled out a handful of purity bombs.

"I would put them in as quickly as possible if I were you," Angeline said as Angelo extended his hand toward the hole.

The demon soldiers quickly stopped pounding on the force field and readied their battle-axes. Each of the demons desired to cut off Angelo's hand.

The purity bombs floated out of Angelo's hand, entered the hole and glowed brightly.

"You didn't really think I would let you put your hand in there, did you?" Angeline asked as the force field began to shrink.

The demon soldiers began pounding harder on the force field until they could pound no more as the force field encased them like shrink wrap.

Angeline waved her hands in the air and the armor of the demon soldiers passed through the force field.

As she lowered the armor to the ground with her telekinesis, the purity bombs made contact with the demon soldiers' skin, ignited them and burned them to ashes.

"You've got to show me how you do that," Angelo said.

"Takes a lot of time and practice," Angeline said.

"You'll have to teach it to me another time," Angelo said as he looked down at the street and saw a group of people screaming while running from armored demon soldiers and demon dogs.

"Let's get to work," Angelo said as he flew down to Union Avenue, pulled out his sword and sliced through four demons with a single stroke. "Let's make our way up and down the streets downtown and meet back up at the library in about 30 minutes. Keep your eyes open for whomever or whatever is responsible for this."

"Okay," Angeline said into her earpiece as she ran down Beale Street at super speed down the street. "If you find the source of the problem, contact me and we'll handle it together."

Angelo landed in front of the library with about a minute to spare and found 20 demons pounding on the doors of the library. He could hear the library patrons screaming for help as he quietly walked up the steps behind the demons.

Angelo slowly pulled out his sword and was about to slice his blade through the demons when several purity bombs fell from the sky.

Eleven of the demons were hit by the bombs and burst into flames and ashes instantly. The remaining demons tried to scurry away, but a man, descending from a rope on the roof of the library and holding a glowing white staff in his right hand, destroyed the demons with the staff in a few quick moves.

"Good thing I was here or you would have let them get away," the man said as he walked through the vapors coming from the piles of ashes.

"Jeff?" Angelo asked, recognizing the man's voice. "How? Where did you come from?"

"Jeff?" Angeline asked as she landed beside Angelo. "How did you get here?"

"We got here the same way you two did," Wiseman J said as he slid down a rope attached to the roof.

"Through the portal," Jeff said.

"We saw it turn red after you two entered…" Wiseman J said.

"We didn't see anything," Angeline said. "We've been home for about an hour and all of this started happening almost as soon as we arrived back."

"An hour?" Jeff asked. "You're telling us that you just left New…I mean, Dark Earth an hour ago?"

"Yes and this…," Angelo said as he waved his hand around in a circle toward the demons flying around in the air and the tornadoes spinning around in the distance. "All of this…literally just happened."

Jeff gave Wiseman J a concerned look, but Wiseman J didn't lose his composure.

"We need to find out who or what is responsible for this," Wiseman J said as he walked to a nearby SUV. "Jeff, alter the headlights while I hotwire this vehicle."

"We haven't seen or encountered anything or anyone we would consider being able to cause this," Angelo said. "We've only been fighting a bunch of armored and unarmored demons and a very large dragon."

"But, it has all the markings of you-know-who," Angeline said.

Wiseman J, Jeff and Angelo stared at Angeline.

"What? It has to be said. What if he isn't dead? Who else could do this? Who would want to?"

Angeline waited for someone to respond but it took a minute for Angelo to do so.

"Then…we have to find him if he is alive," Angelo said. "And I pray to God he isn't."

"And if it's not him," Jeff said, "We have to find out who or what it is and end this quickly. Remember that

Wiseman J and I have seen and experienced this before. It's just the beginning and the longer it goes on, the harder it will be to stop."

Loud explosions, from within the tornadoes that stood near the barrier, began echoing throughout the sky. Flashes of blue light also came from within the tornadoes and large, dark figures shot out of the tornadoes with each flash and explosion.

The heroes watched as the figures flew closer and closer to the area they stood in.

"More dragons," Angeline said.

"The tornadoes have portals in them," Angelo said.

"You have to find a way to close them," Wiseman J said as he connected wires in the SUV. "Jeff can handle the demons in this area."

"Well, I'll destroy the tornadoes and close the portals with my force fields while you slay the dragons, Angelo," Angeline said as she rose into the sky.

Angelo followed, unsheathing his sword. "Let's do it. We'll be back soon, you two. Call us if you need us."

Jeff pulled an earpiece from his duffel bag and placed it in his ear. "Will do. Be careful up there."

Angelo and Angeline nodded as they flew higher into the sky and out of sight.

Jeff opened the passenger side door and stared at Wiseman J as he started the SUV.

"What?" Wiseman J asked.

"J, what's going on here?"

"You mean concerning the time?"

"That and what's happening to this city at the current moment."

"I have no idea, Jeff, but I think..."

The ground suddenly exploded open several feet away from Wiseman J and Jeff. The smell of sulfur floated toward them and intense heat made the gravel crackle.

"Guys," Jeff said as he touched his earpiece. "I think you need to get back here, ASAP."

Jeff hopped into the SUV as Wiseman J sped away, honking at people to flee the area.

"GET OUT OF HERE!" Wiseman J screamed. "Run. Get as far away as you can."

A second explosion several feet in front of the SUV caused Wiseman J to stop the vehicle. Both he and Jeff jumped out the SUV as a large piece of pavement landed on top of it.

"All that hard work gone to waste," Jeff said.

"That's the least of our troubles," Wiseman J said. "Look around."

Jeff slowly pulled out his collapsible white staff and twirled it around in circles as he walked around Wiseman J. "Stay where you are, J. I've got this."

Demons soldiers marched out from around the sides of the buildings on the block. Demon dogs leapt out of the giant, flaming holes in the streets and snarled as they made their way toward Wiseman J and Jeff.

"Great," Jeff said. "Now there are hellholes."

Wiseman J reached into his pocket and pulled out an earpiece. "Angelo and Angeline, we need your help immediately. I think the someone or something responsible for this destruction is about to make an appearance."

"I've got three more portals to close," Angeline said. "I'll be there in about three minutes."

"I've got three dragons, all heading in different directions," Angelo said. "It might take me a little longer to get there, but I'll get there as fast as I can."

Jeff looked back at Wiseman J. "I guess we're on our own for now."

Jeff pulled at the center of his staff with both hands, pulling the glowing weapon apart, and forming two new staffs. He tossed one to Wiseman J.

"I hope you can keep up, old man," Jeff said as he began taking out demon soldiers.

Wiseman J grinned. "I did have a hand in teaching you how to fight," he said as he destroyed three demon dogs.

"Yeah, but that was so long ago," Jeff said.

"Not that long ago," Wiseman J said.

"Well, regardless of how long we've fought creatures like these, I sure hope Angelo and Angeline get here soon," Jeff said.

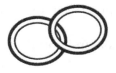

Angelo flew swiftly behind the large black and red dragon that was trying its hardest to get away.

"You're making this harder on yourself," Angelo shouted to the dragon. "All of your buddies are gone. It's time to join them in the pits of hell."

The dragon flapped its wings harder and shot up into the sky, toward the center of the barrier over Memphis.

Angelo was inches away from grabbing the dragon's tail when the dragon, with his wings close by his side, dove toward the city and flew along a row of tall buildings.

"Slick rascal," Angelo said as he flipped backwards in the sky and dove after the dragon. "Angeline, where are you?"

"Flying above Riverside Drive," Angeline said. "I just closed the last portal and the tornadoes are gone. How's the dragon-slaying going?"

"My last one turned out to be a smart one," Angelo said. "But, I'm smarter. I have a plan and I think it can help Jeff and Wiseman J out of their current predicament."

"Just tell me what you need me to do," Angeline said.

Jeff and Wiseman J continued to fight against the hundreds of demon soldiers and demon dogs that stood in the street in front of the library.

"Tired yet, old man?" Jeff asked Wiseman J.

"Not if you aren't," Wiseman J said. "I may not be as young as you, but I still have persistence and determination. That's more than enough to keep this body going…at least until Angelo and Angeline get here."

"Guys, where are you?" Jeff asked into his earpiece. "We need you right now."

"We're very close," Angeline said. "In fact, I'm right above you. You guys should run up the library steps and get as close to the building as you can. On my mark…"

Wiseman J and Jeff continued fighting and steadied themselves to run.

"3...2...now!"

Wiseman J and Jeff raced up the steps and pressed their backs against the library wall.

Suddenly, the dragon Angelo had been chasing flew awkwardly down the street. A glowing purple force field formed around the dragon and slammed into the demon soldiers and demon dogs below.

Angelo hovered over the dragon and began spinning in the air. He pulled out several purity bombs and crushed them in his hands.

The purity dust showered down on the dragon and the remaining demon dogs and demon soldiers, slowly igniting their skin and engulfing them in flames.

The creatures' screams became silent as their bodies turned into ashes.

Angelo and Angeline high-fived each other and landed in front of Jeff and Wiseman J.

The library staff and patrons ran out of the building cheering the heroes.

"That was the most amazing thing I've ever seen," said a woman who stood next to a man who had filmed the entire event with his camera. "My name is Jennifer Cole and this is my husband Neil. Who are you?"

"I'm Angeline and this is Angelo. We are S.O.L.A.D."

"S.O.L.A.D.?" Jennifer asked. "What does that mean?"

"Soldiers of Light Against Darkness," Angelo said.

"And who are they?" Neil asked, pointing to Wiseman J and Jeff.

"Those are our friends, Wiseman J and Jeff," Angeline said.

"Where did you all come from?" Jennifer asked.

"Well, it's a long story," Angeline said. "We are from…"

The ground shook violently before Angeline could finish what she was saying.

"It's an earthquake," one of the librarians said.

Angelo and Angeline looked at the street where the ashes of the dragon and the demons sat.

The ground continued to shake as the ashes shot into the air and back down to the street and formed a large tornado.

"Everyone, get back inside," Angelo said. "That goes for you and Jeff too, Wiseman J."

The librarians and patrons raced inside.

"Neil, they meant us too," Jennifer said to her husband.

"But…"

"Now, Neil!"

Wiseman J followed Jennifer and Neil into the library, but Jeff remained outside with Angelo and Angeline.

"Jeff, go inside," Angelo said.

"No," Jeff said. "I'm not a sidekick. I'm a hero, just like the two of you. In fact, I've been doing this a lot longer than you two have."

"Don't do this now," Angelo said.

"I'm staying to help you two and that's that," Jeff said as he walked down the steps to Angelo and Angeline.

"Ok," Angeline said, motioning for Angelo to stay calm and not get upset. "Let's just work together and put an end to this."

As the ashes slowed down and started to fall to the ground, the heroes could see six figures forming within the dwindling tornado.

The two figures on the ends were clearly male, one large, tall and muscular and the other tall and slender. Between them stood three female figures, a little shorter and who appeared to be floating off the ground. A sixth figure stood a foot behind them.

"Belicista," Jeff said, recognizing the large, tall, muscular figure. "I don't know who the others are, but I know without a doubt that's him. He's responsible for this."

No, he isn't, a voice said from within the minds of Angelo, Angeline and Jeff. *I am.*

The voice telepathically came from the sixth figure.

"You're dead," Angelo said. "I killed you and I watched you burn into nothing inside that volcano."

The ashes ceased falling as the sixth figure walked past the others. The figure was hooded and except for burning, red eyes, appeared to have a featureless, black face.

Yet…here…I…the Demon Master…am.

Tyrone Tony Reed Jr.

3

Speaking Evil

"What do you want, Demon Master?" Angeline asked as she took her bow out and placed three arrows on the line. "Revenge? To rule our world because we liberated yours?"

You always were a smart woman, the Demon Master said telepathically as his eyes glowed.

"You can't have our world," Angelo said as he walked down the steps to confront the Demon Master. "You have no right to be here or to seek revenge. What you did to your world was wrong. You had the power to save it and you destroyed it."

Just like you will...eventually.

"You're wrong," Angelo said. "I'm nothing like you."

"Why are you acting like you know us?" Angeline asked the Demon Master.

You didn't tell her...did you? The Demon Master asked Angelo.

"Tell me what?" Angeline said as she looked at Angelo.

"Don't listen to that devil," Wiseman J said as he walked down the steps and stood beside Jeff and Angeline. "He's a manipulator and a trickster."

Takes one...to know one.

"I've had enough of this," Jeff said as he tossed several purity bombs at the Demon Master and his lieutenants. "Time for you all to die."

The Demon Master and his lieutenants stood in place and didn't even flinch as their skin crackled and healed.

Belicista held his right hand out and a giant battle-axe appeared. He quickly flung the battle-axe into a nearby wooden telephone pole.

Our turn, the Demon Master said.

The Demon Master waved his hand toward the telephone pole and the pole exploded, creating several, six-foot long, wooden-spears. The spears hovered in the air for a few seconds and turned toward Angelo and the others.

As the Demon Master telekinetically sent the spears flying in the heroes' direction, Angeline quickly put up a force field around the heroes, but not before Angelo was impaled in the stomach by three of the spears.

Angelo fell to his knees as his clothing became soaked with blood from his lower back and lower front.

"ANGELO!" Angeline shouted as she began to let her force field drop.

"Keep…your…shield…up," Angelo said as a puddle of blood formed around him. "Stay…back. Drop…shield…when…I…say…so."

Angelo tried with all his might to concentrate on the wooden spears sticking out of his body and not the pain he was feeling or how light-headed he was becoming.

But, the Demon Master was still taunting Angelo telepathically. *You're going to die, boy. Don't fight it and don't fight me. Just go to sleep and you won't have to be in pain anymore.*

Flames leapt high into the air from the hellholes at the ends of the street. Every few seconds, a group of five demon soldiers appeared and began marching toward Angeline's force field.

The demon soldiers pounded on the force field with their hands and their weapons.

"Angelo, whatever you have planned, you need to do it quickly," Angeline said as sweat ran down her face.

"These demons are a lot stronger than the ones we faced earlier."

"Just…a…few…more…seconds," Angelo said as he began to glow white and felt the spears move inside him.

Angelo willed himself to stand up, held his arms out as his sides and yelled, "NOW!"

Angeline dropped her force field and the glowing white, wooden spears shot out of Angelo's stomach at super speed and flew around the heroes. The demon soldiers were pulled into the glowing, white vortex the flying spears had created and were instantly destroyed.

The Demon Master stepped behind his lieutenants as the vortex grew and more demon soldiers were pulled into it.

More and more soldiers leapt out of the hellholes as the vortex continued to twirl.

"You have to close the hellholes," Wiseman J said to Angeline.

"I...got...it," Angeline said.

The vortex dissipated as two of the glowing spears each hovered over a hellhole and twirled like the giant blade of an industrial fan.

The flames of the hellhole were snuffed out and the demons inside were forced back into the closing portals of the hellholes as the winds blew them down.

A loud clap came from above that echoed through the air and sounded like thunder. The spears exploded into tiny pieces and formed a barrier over the hellholes. Bright, white light shined over the barriers and the hellholes closed up.

The light went out and only one spear remained. It hovered over the Demon Master and his lieutenants, who were visibly frightened.

The last spear exploded in the air and glowing, white shrapnel took out the remaining demon soldiers in the immediate area.

When the last of the vapors dissipated and the last of the ashes fell to the ground, Angelo and the other heroes saw a red force field around the Demon Master and his lieutenants.

This is not over, boy, the Demon Master said as he and his lieutenants disappeared. *Enjoy your last hours alive, trying to save lives that will ultimately belong to me.*

The Demon Master's giant red eyes appeared over the city and looked down at the heroes. *I'm going to take away everything that is important to you, Angelo and Angeline. So fight as long as you can. But, this city...this world...will be mine.*

Angelo dropped onto the steps of the library and took a deep breath. "Glad that's over."

Angeline ran to his side and looked at his wounds. "Are you okay?" she asked as the last of the blood stains on Angelo's clothes disappeared.

"My insides are intact and the bleeding has stopped," Angelo said. "The only things bothering me right now are the aches I feel where the spears shot through."

"How did you do that thing with the spears?" Angeline asked.

"And that thunderclap that made them explode and close the hellholes?" Jeff asked.

Angelo shrugged.

"It wasn't me," he said. "I thought Angeline did it."

Angeline shook her head.

Jeff smiled as he looked up.

"You guys know what this means, right?" he asked. "Someone up there is looking out for us."

"That goes without saying, Jeff," Wiseman J said before look over to Angelo. "Do you need to rest a while longer? There doesn't appear to be any immediate danger in the area."

Before Angelo could answer, the heroes heard screams and explosions echoing from behind the buildings in front of them.

"Sounds like trouble," Jeff said as he reconnected his collapsible staff. "Angeline and I can handle them while you stay here with Angelo."

"No," Angelo said as he floated off the steps and grabbed his sword. "We're doing this together. I'll be fine. I'm already feeling better. Besides, we have to stop the Demon Master before he turns our world into Dark Earth."

"We're not going to let that happen," Jeff said.

Angelo rose higher into the air and flew toward the buildings.

"Then let's go be the heroes we are and save the day."

4

Angelic Rescues

Wiseman J and Jeff stood at opposite ends of a high-rise building, using binoculars to look around the city of Memphis.

"I should be down there with Angelo and Angeline," Jeff said. "Instead, I'm up here with you, telling them where the action is."

"Patience, Jeff," Wiseman J said. "They can clear the streets quicker and fight longer than you can, and I might need to send you to areas they are too busy to get to."

Jeff shook his head. "A legendary hero, reduced to backup."

Wiseman J sighed. "Pride cometh before a fall."

"I've already fallen," Jeff said as he reached into his duffel bag and pulled out two needles, which were filled with white, glowing, shimmering substances. "And I might have to pay for it the rest of my life."

Jeff injected the substances into his arm and quickly grabbed the injection site.

Wiseman J started to move toward Jeff, but Jeff held his hand up toward Wiseman J.

"Wait, J," Jeff said as he fell to his knees and his body began to glow white. "It just needs a few seconds to work."

Jeff growled as his blue eyes turned orange, then white, and then back to blue as his body stopped glowing white.

"Are you alright?" Wiseman J asked as he helped Jeff stand. "Is that supposed to happen?"

"After 'he' came up with the serum to keep Monstrosity at bay and Jesheena synthesized it, we tested it as quickly as we could," Jeff said. "Jesheena tried to help me and I ended up throwing her across the room. Good thing 'he" was there to run at super speed and keep her from being injured."

Wiseman J shook his head. "I'm sorry. I didn't know it was that bad."

"It wasn't until a few weeks ago when Jesheena told me I would have to double my dosage," Jeff said. "Seems Monstrosity doesn't want to be silenced."

Wiseman J patted Jeff on the back. "We'll find a way to permanently rid you of that monster."

"That's just it, J," Jeff said. "I am that monster. He's my anger, hate, pride, selfishness and everything evil inside of me. He's something I'll probably battle with for the rest of my life. But, I won't lose the war inside myself and we won't lose this battle we are currently fighting."

Wiseman J smiled. "You're absolutely right."

Jeff walked over to the edge of the rooftop and looked through his binoculars. Through them, he could see Angeline fighting a group of demon soldiers and demon dogs at the intersection of Union Avenue and South Front Street.

"Angeline is doing pretty good clearing the area she's in," Jeff said. "How's the demon-slayer doing?"

Wiseman J looked through his binoculars and spotted Angelo rescuing people from burning buildings on Beale Street.

"Angelo's doing great also," Wiseman J said. "Melanie give him that nickname?"

"Yep," Jeff said. He lowered his binoculars and turned to his mentor. "J, I've been thinking…Angelo and Angeline deserve to know…everything, and I mean everything, that's happened in the year that they left our world. If it weren't for them… if Angelo hadn't sent 'him' to us from his and Juanita's future… we would never have found…"

"Stop," Wiseman J said. "I need to radio Angelo. There's trouble on Peabody Place."

"But…"

"This is not the time. I agree with you, Jeff, but it has to wait. Especially since for Kevin and Juanita, those things…our past and their future… have yet to occur."

"Angelo, come in."

Angelo had just rescued the last of the people from the fires on Beale Street when he heard Wiseman J's voice in his earpiece.

"Go, Wiseman J."

"There's some heavy activity on Peabody Place. Demon soldiers have some people surrounded, but one woman appears to be fighting back."

Angelo's earpiece beeped.

"Angelo, I'm still busy on Union, but I'll be there in a few minutes,' Angeline said.

There was a brief sound of wind blowing on Angelo's end and seconds later, the sound of Angelo's sword hitting armor.

"Okay," Angelo said as he fought and defeated six demon soldiers at one time. "I'm already there. I'm going to give these folks some room to escape. See you soon."

Angelo walked through the ashes and vapors from the six defeated demon soldiers and checked on the people who had been attacked.

"Are you all okay?" Angelo asked.

"Hi, handsome," said a beautiful African-American woman in a red shirt and blue jeans. She held an axe in one hand while waving for people to run into a building with the other. "My name's Victoria."

"Hello, Victoria. My name is Angelo. Thank you for saving those people."

"You're thanking me?" Victoria asked. "I used this axe against those monsters and it did nothing but buy us some time until you got here."

"It was very brave of you," Angelo said. He felt his heart racing the more he heard the woman speak and the more he stared at her. "I'm sure those people you saved would say you are the one who saved them."

Victoria smiled and hugged Angelo. "You're the real hero. And you are so smart."

"Angelo, I'm finished," Angeline said through Angelo's earpiece. "I'm on my way."

"Okay," Angelo said, briefly turning away from Victoria. "See you in a second."

Angelo turned around and said, "Sorry about that Victoria…" Angelo looked around, but Victoria was gone.

Angelo's heart slowed down and returned to normal. *There was something about that woman. Something very familiar.*

"What's wrong?" asked Angeline while she hovered over Angelo.

"Nothing," Angelo said as he floated into the air next to her. He tapped his earpiece. "Where to next, guys?"

"Law enforcement is holding the demon soldiers and demon dogs at bay for the moment," Wiseman J said. "Come to us so we can talk about our next move."

Gunshots and sirens could be heard all around Memphis as people screamed in fear.

Smoke rose up to the rooftop Wiseman J and Jeff stood on.

"So, what's the plan, Wiseman J?" Angelo asked as he hovered several feet above the two men, throwing basketball-sized purity bombs across the city. The bombs exploded once they hit the streets, destroying the demon soldiers and demon dogs in the immediate area, and allowing people to escape.

"There are so many of them," Angeline said as she hovered beside Angelo. She telekinetically controlled her sais to attack demon soldiers and demon dogs on the streets and smashed other groups of demons with her force fields. "The more demons we destroy, the more appear."

"In other words, this is a waste of time," Jeff said as he twirled his staff.

"No, we're saving lives," Angelo said. "This is our world and there are people we probably know and interact with every day down there who are fighting for their lives. We need to find the Demon Master and make sure we put him down for good."

Wiseman J nodded his head. "I believe we first need to close up the hellholes and make sure they stay close. Then we take out each of the Demon Master's lieutenants and finally face the Demon Master."

"What about the demon soldiers and demon dogs?" Angelo asked. "These people are in danger."

"If we don't take out the Demon Master soon, demon dogs and demon soldiers will be the least of our worries," Wiseman J said. "So, this is how we'll…"

The sound of a Boeing AH-64 Apache helicopter's blades whipping through the smoke filled air startled Wiseman J. A few seconds later, a spotlight shined down on the rooftop, briefly blinding Wiseman J and Jeff.

"What do they want?" Jeff asked.

"THIS IS THE UNITED STATES ARMY," a male voice said through a speaker system on the helicopter. "WE HAVE DETECTED STRANGE ACTIVITY COMING FROM THIS ROOFTOP. HAVE YOU TWO SEEN ANYTHING STRANGE?"

"Besides the demons tearing up the city and eating people?" Jeff asked.

As the smoke blew away, Angelo and Angeline hovered down to the rooftop and landed beside Jeff and Wiseman J.

"Did you see that?" asked Lt. Travis Keynard, one of the helicopter pilots, to his co-pilot, Lt. Sarah Sanders. "FIRE!"

In a split-second, an AGM-114 Hellfire missile roared as it flew from the helicopter and headed for the rooftop.

Angeline quickly created a force field around her and the others, just as the missile hit the rooftop and exploded.

"You see anything, Sanders?" Keynard asked.

"Nothing on radar," Sanders said as she looked out the window. "There's a lot of smoke and fire down there. What were those things? They didn't look like the creatures on the streets. They looked humans."

"When was the last time you heard of a human flying?" Keynard asked. "Last time I checked, they only did that in the comic books and movies."

"Look," Sanders said, pointing down at the rooftop the missile struck. "There's something purple glowing down there."

When the smoke cleared a few seconds later, the pilots could see that most of the buildings top floors were gone and there, hovering were the rooftop had been minutes before, was Angelo, Angeline, Wiseman J and Jeff inside Angeline's force field.

"There they are," Sanders said. "They survived."

"They won't survive this," Keynard said as he fired four more Hellfire missiles at the force field.

"Why are they shooting at us?" Jeff asked.

"Because we are flying in the air," Angelo said.

"We need to get to the streets," Angeline said. "They're less likely to fire missiles down there."

Wiseman J and Jeff held onto Angelo's arms as Angeline opened the bottom of the force field.

"You three go first and I'll follow after those missiles explode against the force field," Angeline said.

Several booms echoed across the downtown area as the missiles hit Angeline's force field. Angelo quickly flew to the streets below, released Wiseman J and Jeff and flew back to Angeline.

"It's time to go," Angelo told her as a second Apache helicopter joined the first helicopter.

"OPEN FIRE," Keynard yelled into his headset to the pilots in the other helicopter.

Machine gunfire from the helicopters tore through the air like a million swarms of killer bees as Angelo scooped Angeline into his arms and shot high into the smoke filled skies.

"Where are they?" Sanders asked Keynard.

"I don't know, but we need to send out their descriptions to law enforcement on the ground," Keynard said. "I think they are the ones responsible for this mess."

Wiseman J and Jeff were standing at the front entrance of The Orpheum Theatre when Angelo and Angeline caught up with them. They landed beside the men and stepped back against the front doors.

"Are you two alright?" Wiseman J asked.

"Yeah," Angeline said. "It just took a few minutes for us to find you two after we led those helicopters away."

"I hate they think we are the enemy," Angelo said, "but we can't worry about it right now."

"I think we are going to have to," Angeline said as two tanks and several trucks blocked off the intersections of Beale Street and South Main Street and Linden Avenue and South Main Street.

Members of the Memphis Police Department, Shelby County Sheriff's Office, Tennessee Bureau of Investigation, U.S. Secret Service, Tennessee Highway Patrol, U.S. Marshal's Service and the Department of

Homeland Security had their weapons pointed at the heroes.

"DROP YOUR WEAPONS AND PUT YOUR HANDS IN THE AIR," a male voice said from the large speakers on a black van, which sat across the street from them. "THIS IS MEMPHIS POLICE CHIEF MARCUS GRAYSON AND WE WANT TO END THIS WITHOUT ANYMORE LIVES BEING LOST."

Angeline sighed. "Great. Dad would have to be leading the charge," she said to Angelo.

"Too bad you can't just tell him who you are and that we are the good guys," Jeff said.

"We can at least tell them we are the good guys," Angelo said as he raised his hands into the air and began walking toward the van.

Angeline followed Angelo's lead, raising her hands and walking a few steps behind him.

"STOP RIGHT THERE," Marcus said, as the law enforcement officers surrounding Angelo and Angeline cocked their weapons. "YOU TWO TAKE ANOTHER STEP AND WE WILL OPEN FIRE."

"Okay," Angelo said as he stopped walking and stood in the middle of South Main Street. "My name is Angelo, Chief Grayson, and this is my partner, Angeline. We are not your enemy. We are here to help."

"YOU ARE RESPONSIBLE FOR THIS," Grayson said.

"No, we aren't," Angeline said. "We are trying to stop this attack before there is no one left to save and this city is destroyed."

"IF YOU ARE TELLING THE TRUTH, THEN YOU WILL SURRENDER," Grayson said. "PUT YOUR WEAPONS ON THE GROUND, PUT YOUR

HANDS ON YOUR HEAD AND GET DOWN ON

THE GROUND. NOW!"

Angelo and Angeline looked back at Wiseman J and

Jeff and the men nodded to them that they would

comply with Grayson's orders.

Angeline placed her sais and her quiver on the

ground as Angelo placed his sword, which still sat in its

sheathe, on the ground beside Angeline's weapons.

They both put their hands on the back of their heads

and began to get down on the ground as Jeff and

Wiseman J did the same.

The heroes were inches away from lying completely

on the ground when Jeff noticed glowing objects on the

inside of the front glass doors of the Orpheum Theatre.

"Guys…," Jeff said. "We're about to have unwanted

company."

Angelo and Angeline heard what Jeff had said through their earpieces and had quickly looked back at the Orpheum Theatre.

"GET DOWN," Angelo and Angeline said to the law enforcement officers as they reached for their weapons.

"THEY'RE REACHING FOR THEIR WEAPONS," Grayson said. "OPEN FIRE!"

Angelo and Angeline quickly held their hands out in front of themselves and their shields appeared and expanded as rounds of ammunition were fired in their direction.

They scooted back toward Wiseman J and Jeff.

"Well, that didn't go well," Angelo said.

"And now it's about to get worst," Jeff said as the front doors of the Orpheum Theatre exploded and 66 winged demon soldiers flew out and attacked the law enforcement officers.

Some of the demon soldiers lunged for the necks of the officers, biting and gulping down huge chunks of flesh and muscles and nearly decapitating the officers, while other demon soldiers ripped off the officers' arms and used their weapons against them.

But, there was one thing all the attacking demons had in common: they all had sadistic grins on their faces as they maimed and eviscerated the officers.

"Here," Angelo said as he gave his shield to Jeff. "You and Wiseman J go through the theatre and go out the back. You'll come out onto Front Street. Take that street south and get to the Amtrak Station. We'll meet you two there as soon as we're finished here."

"Ok," Jeff said as he pulled out his collapsible staff and strapped Angelo's shield onto his left arm. "Be careful you two."

Tyrone Tony Reed Jr.

5

Friends, Not Foes

Angeline and Angelo both moved at super speed as they maneuvered past bullets and destroyed the demon soldiers. They moved so fast that, to them, the bullets seemed to be frozen in air.

The demon soldiers weren't as fast and were surprised when law enforcement officers were suddenly freed from their grasps by unseen forces.

Seconds later, the rescued law enforcement officers, who were moments before, about to be torn apart and eaten, found themselves in the front parking lot of the Memphis, Light, Gas and Water building on South 2nd

Street. A minute later, all of their weapons appeared in a pile before them.

"How did we get here?" one officer asked Grayson.

"I don't know," Grayson said. "But, I think we were carried here by that woman with the arrows and that man with the sword."

Nearly two dozen demon soldiers remained in front of the Orpheum Theatre after Angelo and Angeline had finished rescuing the law enforcement officers and finally slowed down enough so the demon soldiers could see them.

"Where's your master?" asked Angelo as he pulled out his Sword of Faith.

"Ask...Titan,' one of the demon soldiers said.

"What's a Titan?" Angeline asked.

"I AM TITAN!" a loud, deep voice yelled.

A giant demon soldier walked up from behind a line of smaller demon soldiers and puffed up his chest and pointed his battle-axe toward Angelo.

"Don't worry about our master," Titan said. "You'll be defeated by me before you can get to him."

Angelo looked back at Angeline and smiled.

"He's a biggun," Angeline told Angelo.

"He is," Angelo said as he put his sword back in its sheathe and stepped back. "He's all yours."

Angeline threw her quiver and sais on the ground. She cracked her knuckles and tilted her head from side to side as she walked up to Titan.

He looked past her and directly at Angelo.

"COWARD," Titan said in a loud voice that sounded like large stones being scraped together. "You let this weak woman fight for you?"

The smaller demon soldiers laughed but quickly stopped when Angelo started laughing.

"Hey, just remember you asked for what's about to come," Angelo said.

Titan looked down on Angeline and snarled. "What are *you* going to do, little lady?"

"First, he doesn't *let* me do anything," Angeline said as she flew up to Titan's face and uppercutted him. The impact of the punch sent him crashing into the Orpheum Theatre's lighted sign.

"Second, I'm stronger than you think I am," Angeline said as Titan fell to the ground and the Orpheum sign fell on top of him.

The smaller demon soldiers started toward Angeline, but Angelo quickly pulled out his sword as his eyes glowed white behind his shades.

"That's far enough, fellas," Angelo said. "Unless you're eager to be next?"

The smaller demon soldiers backed away.

Suddenly, the Orpheum Theatre sign flew toward Angeline and Angelo. It broken into several large pieces before it could reach them as it crashed into Angeline's invisible force field.

"That wasn't fair or nice," Angeline said. "You shouldn't try to kill a lady with a sign when she's not looking."

Titan growled loudly as he ran toward Angelo and Angeline.

"I got him," Angeline said.

Titan swung at Angeline with his right fist, but Angeline stepped to her left at super speed, caught his arm and quickly spun him around several times. After several spins, she let Titan go and he flew into a line of smaller demon soldiers with such force that the smaller demon soldiers burst into flames and burned into ashes.

Angelo high-fived Angeline as he walked past her and stood once again behind her.

The remaining demon soldiers charged at Angeline, but didn't notice her sais levitating off the ground and spinning in a circle. Before they could reach her, Angeline's sais had shot through them and ignited them. A few seconds later, several piles of ashes surrounded Angeline.

"You're amazing," Angelo said as he picked up Angeline's quiver and handed it to her.

"She certainly is," Grayson said as he and several Memphis police officers approached the heroes. "Who are you two supposed to be?"

As Angelo opened his mouth to speak, Grayson and the other officers pulled out their guns and pointed them toward the heroes.

"Not again," Angelo said as he and Angeline put their hands behind their heads. "We are the good guys."

"We know that," Grayson said, "But, he isn't."

Angelo and Angeline turned around and saw Titan at the end of the intersection of Beale Street and South Main Street. He breathed heavily as several cuts across his body oozed blood.

Titan grabbed a light pole and bared his teeth.

"No, he's definitely not with us," Angeline said.

"Good," Grayson said. "OPEN FIRE!"

Bullets whizzed over Angelo and Angeline's heads toward Titan. The bullets found their target but he didn't flinch as the bullets went through his body.

Titan roared and ran toward the heroes and the officers with great speed.

"GET BACK," Angeline screamed as she threw up a force field between herself and Titan.

Titan bashed the light pole against the force field, causing Angeline to strain under the pressure.

Seeing Angeline under distress, Angelo, with sword in hand, flew over the force field and lunged at Titan.

He swatted Angelo into the second floor of the Orpheum Theatre.

"You wanted me to face her," Titan said, "so, she's all mine."

Angeline gritted her teeth as she pushed her hands out in front of herself, causing the force field to slam into Titan.

Titan, caught off-guard, stumbled backwards but quickly regained his composure and began bashing the force field again, with double the strength.

"Angelo," Angeline said into her earpiece. "I need your help now. I can't keep this up much longer."

Angeline's force field began to crack as Titan continued to pound steadily on it.

"I'm coming for you, girl," Titan said. He licked his lips, smiled and rolled his eyes into the back of his head. "I can't wait to devour you."

A "boom" echoed across the street as an army tank fired a high explosive incendiary/armor piercing ammunition (HEIAP) at Titan. A second "boom" followed as the ammunition hit him in the back.

Angeline's force field shattered as Titan began to burn and burst into flames.

"Thanks," Angeline said to the tanker as she dropped to ground.

Titan stood still as flames wrapped around his body and continued to intensify.

The officers cheered as Grayson helped Angeline to her feet.

"Are you all right?" he asked as she looked up at the hole in the second floor of the Orpheum Theatre.

Angeline watched as Angelo stood up, floated out of the hole and landed next to her and Grayson.

"I am now," Angeline said.

Angelo and Angeline looked at Titan, who still hadn't burnt into ashes.

"Something's wrong," Angelo said as he motioned for Angeline, Grayson and the officers to back away. "No screams or moans and no disintegration."

Before Angelo could say another word, Titan held his left arm out and opened his left hand.

The flames that wrapped around his body seeped into his pours and into his nostrils, mouth, eyes and ears.

When the flames were gone, there stood Titan, completely healed and even taller, with flames flickering from within his eyes.

"Thanks for the upgrade," he said as a red fireball formed in his left hand.

Titan turned away from the heroes and threw the fireball at the tank. The tank exploded and everyone inside was killed.

Titan laughed as he formed two more fireballs in his hands and fired them toward the officers.

Angelo ran at super speed, using his sword to hitting the fireballs high into the sky. Angeline formed force fields around the fireballs, snuffing out the flames.

"There's more where that came from," Titan said as flames leapt out of his mouth with each word he spoke.

The flames shot out, like a flamethrower, from Titan's mouth and eyes toward Angelo and Angeline.

The heroes dodged the attack, flew into the sky and hovered over Titan.

"Exactly where I want you," Titan said as he held his hand out toward the officers and continued to look up at the heroes.

Flames shot out of Titan's hands and burned several officers, who had begun shooting at him.

Angeline pulled the Orpheum Theatre's marquee sign from the front of the building and slammed it into

Titan. She slammed it into him several more times, at super speed, before slamming it on him a final time.

As she checked on the burnt officers, the marquee sign flew up into the air, hitting Angelo. The sign fell down a few feet behind the burning tank as Titan stood up and laughed.

Angelo slammed into Titan and began punching him at super speed.

"This…won't…stop…me," Titan said between each of Angelo's punches. He heated his body up, creating a heat barrier around himself.

"That might not," Angeline said as she ripped a fire hydrant out of the ground and used her shield to shoot Titan with water. "But, this could."

The water soaked Titan as Angelo reached into a pouch on his belt.

Angeline squeezed the water main closed and watched as Titan tried to reignite the fire that had moments ago resided inside him.

"Cooler heads prevailed," Angelo said as he pulled out a single purity bomb and let it fall into the puddle of water Titan stood in.

The purity bomb shook and shined before it burnt out and dissolved.

Titan laughed. "What was that supposed to do? Scare me? It didn't even do what it was supposed to do."

"Yes it did," Angelo said as he landed in front of Titan. He pointed to the puddle. "See?"

The puddle turned into a white, sparkling substance and overtook Titan, who fought to break away but couldn't. He involuntarily absorbed the substance until it was completely inside him.

Titan laughed again as his skin ignited and flames wrapped around his body. "I told you it didn't work."

He opened his right hand to create a fireball, but the flames would not obey him anymore. Titan's flesh began to crack and sizzle as his body burned into ashes.

"NOOOOOOOOOOOOOOOOOOOOOOOOOOO," Titan screamed.

A gust of wind blew Titan's ashes past Angelo, Angeline and down South Main Street.

Claps and cheers surrounded the heroes as the law enforcement officers approached them.

"I still don't know who you two are, but we owe you two our lives," Grayson said.

"No, you don't," Angelo said. "It's our duty to serve and protect, just as it is yours."

"My name is Angeline and his name is Angelo," Angeline said as she shook Grayson's hand. *I sure hope dad doesn't recognize me.*

"I wish I could say it is a pleasure to meet you both, but under the present conditions, I think the presence of you two confirms my fears that this is something we can't handle," Grayson said.

Lightning began striking the street and the officers ran for cover.

Angelo and Angeline, followed by Grayson and a few officers, ran to the covered parking lot of the Tri-State Bank of Memphis.

"Now it's storming," Grayson said. "That's just great."

Angeline watched the lightning strikes, which had started lasting longer and hitting the street more frequently.

"That isn't normal lightning," Angeline said.

As the streets around them continued to be struck, the ground shook and sounded as if it were groaning.

Suddenly, the lightning stopped and the ground ceased its shaking.

"Please, stay here," Angeline told the officers. "Let us make sure everything is all right."

Angelo and Angeline were walking down Beale Street when a huge, red lightning bolt struck the Elvis Presley statue in Elvis Presley Plaza. The ground exploded next to the statue and after a few seconds, the lightning stopped again.

When the dust from the explosion cleared, a woman, with brown hair and red eyes, dressed in an orange outfit, sat in front of the statue.

"Well, that was dramatic," the woman said. "But, every king deserves a queen and every queen deserves an army."

About 50 law enforcement officers simultaneously pulled out their weapons and pointed them at the woman.

The woman laughed and waved her right hand in the air, as if she were beckoning someone one to come down.

Suddenly, five bolts of lightning shot down from the sky and struck the ground, which exploded and sizzled as five, giant demon soldiers, who looked like they were made of stone, stepped out.

The demon soldiers were as fast as lightning and before Angelo and Angeline could react, they had killed all 50 law enforcement officers. After the massacre, the demon soldiers kneeled before their queen.

The woman stared at Angelo and Angeline and grinned.

"Did I mention my name is Destruction and that I'm here to destroy everything and everyone in sight?"

6

Extinguishing Hope

Angeline quickly formed a force field, encasing her, Angelo, Destruction and Destruction's demon soldiers inside it.

"What is this?" Destruction muttered as an unpleasant look formed on her face.

"No way out," Angeline said as she pulled out her bow and arrows and shot the five demon soldiers one by one.

Angelo ran at super speed and pulled out his sword as he made his way toward Destruction.

The ground suddenly collapsed underneath him. Angelo floated out of the crater and as he did, monstrous hands, made of soil, grabbed him and forced him back down as the ground began to close.

"ANGELO!" Angeline screamed as she ran toward him.

A lightning bolt struck Angeline and the impact slammed her into her force field. The force field began to come down and Destruction waved her right hand, which crackled as lightning danced around her fingertips, into the air again.

This time, ten lightning bolts struck the ground and ten, stone demon soldiers stepped out.

Angeline quickly reformed her force field around Destruction and her demon soldiers.

"You can't keep us in here, little girl," Destruction said.

"I'm going to try," Angeline said as she pulled out her sais. "I just have to keep it up long enough to destroy all of you."

Destruction laughed. "Sweetheart, you are greatly outnumbered. You don't stand a chance against us."

Lightning danced around Destruction's body and she grinned as her demon soldiers lined up beside her.

"You see, whatever I can do," Destruction said, "these guys can do also."

Lightning danced around the demon soldiers and lightning sparked outside their eyes.

"Ready," Destruction said as she gestured her hands to resemble pistols toward Angeline. "Aim."

Destruction's demon soldiers mimicked her, resembling a firing squad aiming at the target they were about to execute.

Angeline held her right hand out and her shield appeared as Destruction said, "Fire."

Streaks of lightning shot from the hands of Destruction and her demon soldiers and struck Angeline's shield.

Thunder boomed as the demons continue to shoot lightning at Angeline.

Every time their lightning bolts struck Angeline's shield, the force field would open up a little more.

So hard...to concentrate, Angeline thought. *Can't let...them get out...*

Angeline kneeled and threw one of her sais into the chest of one of the demon soldiers as they were about to shoot more lightning bolts at her.

The demon soldier grabbed the sai and yanked it out. The demon soldier fell to the ground and screamed as white lightning exploded from its body and struck three other demon soldiers, who also screamed and fell to the ground. Seconds later, the demon soldiers were ashes.

"That was some trick," Destruction said as she made her way behind the six remaining demon soldiers. She glanced up at the force field and saw that it was forming back together.

"Well, here's another," Angelo said as he burst out of the ground behind Destruction and her demon soldiers. He slashed the soil hands that reached for him and threw several purity bombs at Destruction.

One of her demon soldiers jumped in front of Destruction and shielded her from the purity bombs. The demon soldier instantly ignited and burned into a pile of ashes.

While Destruction was distracted by the demon soldier's death, Angeline dropped her shield and her bow appeared in her hand as the shield disappeared. Angeline quickly fired three purity arrows into the chests of three of the five remaining demon soldiers.

Destruction turned around and screamed as the three demon soldiers burst into flames and burned into ashes.

The two demon soldiers left walked around Destruction, anxiously awaiting Angeline's and Angelo's next attack.

Destruction put her hands on their chests, making the demon soldiers stop.

"There's no need for that, boys," Destruction said.

"You're surrendering?" Angeline asked.

"Sweetheart, get real," Destruction said. "We demons don't give up, especially without a fight and the fight is just beginning."

Destruction grinned as lightning danced across her fingertips and shot into the chest of her demon soldiers. The demon soldiers screamed in pain and then exploded into 50 stone pieces.

Angelo laughed. "Whoops. Looks like whatever you were trying to do didn't work. You just made this easier for us."

Destruction fell to her knees and cried. "I can't go out like this…"

The ground shook and the stone pieces that were once Destruction's demon soldiers rolled next to Angeline's force field.

"And I won't," Destruction said before laughing.

The stone pieces grew into 50 new stone demon soldiers, who began pounding on Angeline's force field.

Angeline grunted as she tried to keep her force field up.

"I got them," Angelo said as he ran at super speed, slicing through the demon soldiers with his sword.

Instead of the demon soldiers igniting and burning into ashes, they crumbled into piles of stones. Moments later, each stone became a new stone demon soldier.

"They're over a hundred of them now," Angeline told Angelo, who was now standing next to her.

"And they can all replicate if we try to destroy them," Angelo said.

"Boys, bring this force field down," Destruction said. "It's time to get out into that big city and do some damage."

The demon soldiers all shouted "AS YOU COMMAND", and pounded on the force field.

It was too much for Angeline, who fell to her knees and held up her hands toward the opening in her force field.

"Too much…" Angeline said as she struggled to keep her force field from opening. The force field began to shatter at the points the demon soldiers were attacking.

"Can you encase each of the demon soldiers into their own force field like you did earlier?" Angelo asked Angeline. "And make the force field so tight around them like they are in plastic wrap?"

"That way they can't move or pound on the force field," Angeline said.

"Right," Angelo said, "And I'll take care of Destruction."

"YOU MEAN, DESTRUCTION WILL TAKE CARE OF YOU," said a booming voice from above the heroes.

Angelo and Angeline looked up to see Destruction had grown into a 20-foot giant. Angeline's force field stretched like putty around the giant demoness.

Before the heroes could move, Destruction had pounded on Angelo several times, picked him up and punched him through the top of the force field. After making a hole, she threw him high into the sky.

"IT WAS A SOUND PLAN," Destruction told Angeline. "YOU JUST DIDN'T ACT QUICKLY ENOUGH."

Destruction kicked Angeline into her force field, knocking Angeline out and causing the remaining parts of the force field to disappear.

"EXCELLENT," Destruction said as she looked down on an unconscious Angeline. "I SHOULD KILL YOU, BUT, MY MASTER HAS COMMANDED ME NOT TO. HOWEVER, I CAN CAUSE YOU A LOT OF PAIN!"

Destruction stepped on Angeline and tried to smear her into the ground like she was putting out a cigarette.

Destruction raised her foot and laughed at the sight of the bruised and bloody Angeline.

"LET'S GO, BOYS," Destruction said. "WE'VE GOT A CITY TO DESTROY!"

"AS YOU COMMAND," the demon soldiers shouted.

Tyrone Tony Reed Jr.

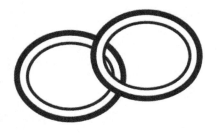

Middle:
Trials & Tribulations

7

Darkness & Destruction

"Angeline? Angeline, are you okay?"

The voice sounded distorted as Angeline rubbed her head and grabbed her ribs. She hurt all over and grunted as broken bones popped back together.

"Are you okay, Angeline?" the voice asked again.

This time she recognized that the voice belonged to Jeff.

"I will be soon," Angeline said as she saw Jeff and Wiseman J looking down at her from the giant hole in the street she laid in. "Just a little groggy. How long have I been out?"

"About 20 minutes," Wiseman J said.

Angeline slowly floated out of the hole and as she did, the bruises on her body began to fade away.

"Man, how I wish I had powers like you two," Jeff said as Angeline landed next to them.

"How is Angelo?" Angeline asked.

"He's over there and unconscious," Wiseman J said, pointing to a nearby crater. "His wounds from our earlier encounter with the Demon Master seemed to have begun bleeding again after he fell from the sky."

"We saw him fall," Jeff said. "And we saw the giant woman leave the area. That's how we found the two of you."

Angeline walked over to the crater, flew down into it, picked up Angelo and flew him out of it. She gently laid him onto an area of grass.

"He's healing up also," Wiseman J said as he saw Angelo's blood-stained clothing start to slowly turn white. "But, it's much slower than you healed up, Angeline."

"Where are Destruction and her army?" Angeline asked, looking around the area.

"You mean the giant woman?" Jeff asked. "She was heading north when she began shrinking."

Angeline heard screams and gunfire in the distance and saw buildings collapsing. The ground also shook violently as explosions occurred in the north part of downtown.

Angeline knelt and rubbed Angelo's cheek.

"Your city needs you, Angeline," Jeff said. "The causalities are increasing. The Army, the FBI, the National Guard and the police…they're all being slaughtered."

Angeline quickly stood up and her bow appeared in right hand.

"My dad…," Angeline said as she floated into the sky. "Watch over Angelo and let him know I need him as soon as he wakes up."

It only took two seconds in super speed for Angeline to fly to the area the gunfire was coming from.

The sky was thick with dust and smoke, but with her super hearing, she could hear her father yelling for officers to get back from several of Destruction's soldiers.

Angeline's super sight kicked in and as she peered through the dust and smoke, she could see small streaks of lightning dancing along the fingertips of several of Destruction's stone demon soldiers.

As she flew down, the demon soldiers shot big bolts of lightning at the police cruisers and tanks in the area.

Angeline quickly created force fields around the officers as explosions shook the area and shattered the windows of nearby windows and vehicles. As she made her way through the explosions, Angeline rapidly fired arrows through each demon soldier.

Flames shot out of the bodies of the demons and engulfed them until nothing but ashes remained.

"Are you all okay?" Angeline asked as she landed in front of Grayson and several other law enforcement officers.

"We are now, thanks to you," Grayson said.

"No, you aren't," Destruction said as she rose out of the rubble of a nearby building. "You killed my soldiers, but I can always make more, better soldiers…ones that can blow things and…people up with their minds."

"GET OUT OF HERE," Angeline screamed at the law enforcement officers as she fired arrows and began firing arrows at Destruction.

Destruction's eyes and hands glowed bright orange as the rubble underneath her slowly joined together to create several 10-feet tall stone demon soldiers with glowing orange eyes.

The stone demon soldiers glowed bright orange as they raised their hands out toward the fleeing law enforcement officers.

The officers stopped in mid-stride and levitated off the ground. Their cruisers and guns followed suit.

Angeline fired arrows at the stone demon soldiers as the cruisers and guns exploded.

Seconds later, the officers' bodies began to expand and their eyes began to bulge.

"STOPPPPP!!!!" Angeline screamed as she continued shooting arrows into the stone demon soldiers.

Even though the arrows hit their targets, the stone demon soldiers continued to use their telekinetic powers to slowly inflate the law enforcement officers.

One of those officers was Grayson. He and his fellow officers gritted their teeth as blood ran from noses, ears and eyes.

Angeline's quiver disappeared from off her back and her bow disappeared from her right hand. She quickly pulled out her sais and ran at super speed. As she did, her bow appeared overhead, with her quiver close by.

One by one, arrows flew out of the quiver, lined up along the bow and fired in rapid succession, as if an invisible person were providing Angeline cover-fire.

But, it was Angeline, using her telekinesis, while she attacked the stone demon soldiers up close and personal.

Angeline rammed her sais into the chests of several stone demon soldiers before they even knew what had hit them.

The law enforcement officers fell to the ground and sighed with relief as the stone demon soldiers exploded into ashes.

"Are you okay, Chief Grayson?" Angeline said as she knelt beside Grayson. She wanted to tell her father that she was really Juanita. And she felt she would have if there hadn't been so many injured officers nearby that could possibly overhear the revelation.

"Yes, I am," Grayson said as he wiped the blood from his face with his sleeve. "We all are, thanks again to you."

"AGAIN…NO…YOU…ARE…NOT!" Destruction screamed as her voice echoed around Angeline and the injured law enforcement officers.

Destruction lunged from the middle floor of a nearby building and telepathically caused all of the buildings around Angeline and the law enforcement officers to explode.

Angeline created a force field around the law enforcement officers as she flew high into the air and slammed into Destruction like a heat-seeking missile.

The impact sent Destruction crashing through the street, into the sewers and several feet into the ground below the sewers.

When Destruction floated out of the ground a few minutes later, she was drenched in sewage and mud. The smile she had been showcasing earlier as she attacked Memphis was now gone and she bared her teeth like an angry animal.

"What, no witty remarks this time, Destruction?" Angeline asked.

Destruction breathed heavily through her teeth as her hands glowed bright orange.

"Okay then," Angeline said. "Let's finish this."

Rapid blasts of orange energy shot from Destruction's hands as she tried to knock Angeline out of the sky.

Angeline weaved between the blasts, inching closer and closer to Destruction. When she was close enough, Angeline uppercutted Destruction, flew at super speed to catch Destruction and tossed her back into the ground.

Destruction shot out of the ground and held her hands toward Angeline. Destruction's hands glowed orange when Angeline jerked back as if she had been hit by an unseen force.

S.O.L.A.D.™: It's Just the Beginning

"You're not the only one with telekinesis," Destruction said as she slammed Angeline around with it.

"And you're not the only one who has mastered it," Angeline said as she hovered in the air and raised her arms out to her sides. As Destruction held her arms out toward Angeline, a purple force field, a few inches away from Angeline's body, began to glow.

Orange explosions appeared around the force field as Destruction tried to use her telekinetic blasts to penetrate Angeline's force field and attack her.

Angeline smiled and continued to hover in the air above Destruction.

"Why are you smiling?" Destruction asked as she physically pounded her hands in the air, an action that was mimicked on Angeline's force field by Destruction's telekinesis.

Angeline laughed, which angered Destruction even more.

"WHAT'S SO FUNNY?" Destruction screamed.

"Those metal beams that are about to slam into you," Angeline said.

"I'm not falling for that," Destruction said.

A large metal beam slammed into the back of Destruction's head knocking her forward, followed by a second large metal beam that hit her in the forehead and slammed her into the buildings below.

"It appears you did," Angeline said as she descended onto the street.

The street underneath Angeline exploded, throwing her back into the air and onto the nearby rooftop of a building.

Angeline rolled off her back, stood up and walked over to the edge. She saw Destruction, hair all over her head, clothes torn, and blood streaming from several deep gashes across her body, staring back at her.

"You…little…,"Destruction snarled. Her heart beat was rapid as she continued took deep breaths.

"Temper, temper," Angeline said. "That's no way for 'royalty' to talk."

Destruction held her right hand out and moved it as if she were crushing something in her hand. "You…die…NOW!"

The building under Angeline shook and crumbled as she flew off it and kicked Destruction in the head.

"STOP…HITTING…ME!" Destruction screamed.

The ground exploded again, knocking back Angeline, who quickly flew through the debris.

Destruction caught Angeline by the neck and slammed her into the ground.

"I was going to let you live long enough to see my master destroy your city," Destruction said as she picked Angeline up and slammed her into the side of a building. "But, you... have gotten... on my... last... nerve."

Destruction tossed Angeline into the building and raised her hand into the air, making the crushing gesture again. "Enjoy your tomb. Sorry I didn't have time to decorate it for you."

The building shook and collapsed on Angeline. Destruction sat down on some rubble and watched as the tall building continued to fall down on her defeated foe.

"It's so beautiful," Destruction said.

Destruction looked around and saw law enforcement officers and other bystanders several feet away. There was a look of shock, fear and dismay on their faces.

Destruction laughed. "Don't worry. I'll make tombs for all of you very soon."

"No, she won't," a female voice said from behind her.

Destruction turned around and her smile quickly disappeared. In front of her stood Angeline, looking perfectly fine after having a building collapse on her.

"Impossible," Destruction said as her hands glowed. She fired several blasts, but Angeline dodged each one.

Destruction screamed and shook her hands in the air erratically. "I... can't... stand... you. And apparently, I can't kill you or seriously hurt you."

Destruction paused and pointed her index finger down the street at the bystanders. "But, I can kill them and I know that will hurt you."

A small ball of orange energy exploded out of Destruction's fingertip and grew larger as it sped toward the bystanders.

"You can't fight me and save them," Destruction said. "Choose wisely."

Angeline, in super speed, flew down the street and step in front of the bystanders, just as the giant ball of energy was about to reach them.

Destruction started to laugh when she saw Angeline jump in front of the blast, but didn't when the ball of energy did not explode.

The ball of energy twirled around, like a ball of fire, inches from Angeline. As she raised her hand toward it, the ball of energy turned white, began moving away from her and shot back down the street.

Destruction ran as fast as she could as the ball of energy, moments before in her control, raced after her.

It...can't end...this way, Destruction thought as she ran and flew off the ground.

But the ball of energy was inches away from striking her down.

With all of her energy, Destruction telekinetically surrounded herself with the gravel beneath her.

Destruction knew she couldn't outrun it and willed the gravel to attach to her body. She turned around to face the ball of energy as it collided into her and exploded.

Dust and gravel flew into the air and landed into a large hole, where Destruction had made her final stand.

Angeline flew over the hole and looked down at the pieces of gravel, that moments before had covered Destruction's body.

"Ashes to ashes, Destruction," Angeline said as cheers erupted from the bystanders down the street.

Angeline ascended high over the city and pressed a button on her earpiece. "Jeff. J. Destruction has been dealt with. How's Angelo?"

8

City of F.E.A.R.
(False Evidence Appearing Real)

The pain that had been shooting throughout Angelo's body suddenly stopped as he opened his eyes. Darkness seemed to surround him as he tried to make out where he was. The smell of sulfur filled his lungs as he stood up and looked around.

Angelo found himself staring at a set of chained doors and instantly realized he was at the entrance of the auditorium of Whitehaven High School, the school Kevin and Juanita were scheduled to graduate from in a few days.

He turned around and saw orange and red lights coming from a giant hellhole on the stage. The lights also revealed to Angelo that he was not alone in the auditorium. He saw people, of all ages, standing in front of the rows of seats and demons hanging along the walls and the ceiling. People and demons also stood at the entrance, but left a single aisle, which led up to the stage, clear for Angelo to walk through.

Angelo's white aura shined brightly as he stood in the aisle and walked toward the stage.

Angelo felt like it was taking him forever to reach the stage and the auditorium seemed to grow as it more demons leapt out of the hellhole and crammed into the packed auditorium.

When Angelo was half-way down the aisle, the people's eyes turned bright red while the demons' eyes turned bright orange and they chanted in unison, "Come, master! Come!"

No one seemed to even notice Angelo as he reached the stairs that led to the stage.

As he walked up the steps, Angelo noticed a large throne sitting behind the hellhole.

And then, in an instant, Angelo's body failed to obey his commands, as if someone else were in control of it.

What's going on? Angelo thought as he walked over to the hellhole, floated backwards and sat on the throne. *I don't want to be here.*

The people and the demons cheered as the white aura around Angelo turned red, Seconds later, his clothes turned into a black and dark red ceremonial robe.

Why are y'all cheering? Angelo thought. *And why can't I speak or move?*

Hellholes exploded open all over the auditorium, killing the people inside and transforming them into demons.

Fear rushed over Angelo as he struggled within himself to make his body move and flee the auditorium.

SOMEBODY...PLEASE HELP ME! Angelo screamed in his mind. *I DON'T WANT TO BE HERE! THIS IS TOO MUCH! GOD...SAVE ME!*

The throne rose high into the air and the auditorium, along with the rest of the high school, exploded into a million pieces.

Armored flying demon soldiers zipped past the throne and destroyed buildings and numerous hellholes could be seen opening from Angelo's bird's eye point-of-view.

As the throne flew through the destroyed streets of Downtown Memphis, it suddenly stopped in front of a mirrored-glassed building.

No...it can't be! Angelo thought. *NOOOOOOOOOOO!*

Sitting on the throne, in the reflection of the glass, was the Demon Master, who laughed wickedly with joy.

"Guys, where are you?" Angeline asked into her earpiece. "Jeff? Wiseman J? Helloooooooo?"

Angeline continued to hover over the area she had defeated Destruction in and looked down at her father, the other law enforcement officers and the bystanders she had saved. She watched as some of the officers and bystanders pointed at her and cheered.

Angeline smiled. *Thank you, Lord for allowing me to have the opportunity to save my father and those like him. He's saved my life so many times and has been there for me. I don't know what I would have done if I had lost him.*

As Angeline turned to fly away, she heard loud explosions beneath her. The shockwave of the explosions tossed her higher into the sky and would have knocked her unconscious if she had not created a force field around herself.

Flames followed the shockwave, wrapping around Angeline's force field as she screamed, "DAD" over and over again.

Tears streamed from Angeline's eyes as she descended into the massive inferno. Her hands shook uncontrollably as she landed six feet below street level in the area where she had last seen her father and the others.

"DAD?" Angeline continued to cry out. "DAD, WHERE ARE YOU?"

Angeline tossed large pieces of rubble high into the air as she searched for her father.

"DAD?" Angeline's screams were so loud that it shook the ground. "PLEASE TELL ME WHERE YOU ARE!"

Angeline continued to search for her father, walking over the charred and dismembered remains of the people she had saved minutes before.

This can't be happening, Angeline thought. *I beat Destruction. I saved them all. I saved dad. He's got to be here...somewhere.*

"DAD?"

As Angeline continued to walk through the site, the flames died out and she could see scattered remains of police uniforms around her. At her feet sat a Memphis Police badge, an insignia patch with five stars and a charred, silver-plated name tag that had "Grayson" engraved into it.

"No...no...no..." The words were barely a whisper as they came out of Angeline's mouth. She fell hard on her knees, picked up her father's name tag and sobbed uncontrollably.

Memories of her father flooded her mind as she realized she would never see him again or hear his voice as he encouraged her to continue being a great young woman.

"I'm so sorry I let you down," Angeline said as she gripped her father's name tag in one hand and held his badge in the other. "You were such…a great…daddy…"

Several feet behind Angeline stood a tall, dark figure of a man. His eyes glowed orange and so did his hands as he held them out toward Angeline.

"That's it, Sweetheart," he said as he walked closer to Angeline. "Let it out. You deserve to weep, especially since this is one of your worst fears come true."

Even though she was crying loudly, Angeline still heard what the man had said. As she continued to cry, she slowly pulled out her sais.

The man, dressed in a black suit and wearing a faded rainbow tie suddenly appeared a few feet in front of her and she instantly knew it was a demon.

He's responsible for this, Angeline thought. *And he's going to pay.*

"Actually, Sweetheart," the demon said, "this is all *your* fault."

He can read my mind?

"Yes, I can," the demon said. "This is your fault. You and your little boyfriend had to play hero and destroy my master's perfect world. So, this is payback. Had you two stayed in your world and left ours alone, your father and others like him wouldn't be dead now."

Angeline wept. "I…didn't…ask to be…a hero."

"Well, it's not too late to stop, Sweetheart," the demon said. "In fact, in a show of good faith, I will not kill anyone else in your world if you will simply give me your ring, renounce your powers and walk away."

"Then you and your master will leave my world and never return?"

"That's the idea," the demon told Angeline. "But, until you do what I've asked, I'm afraid that the killing will continue and that the next victim will be your boyfriend, Angelo."

The Demon Master's laughter trailed off as he tugged at his robe.

I have to…get this…off, Angelo said within the mind of the Demon Master. *This is not…who I am…or who…I…become.*

The Demon Master continued to tug at his robe and eventually, after a few desperate, hard tugs, he yanked it off. There stood Angelo, the Demon Master's robe in hand, floating over a cemetery.

Free at last, Angelo thought as he looked himself over.

Angelo released the robe, letting it fall to the grounds of the cemetery.

Angelo watched as the robe blew in the wind and landed next to a row of graves, heavily adorned with dead flowers.

What is up with that? Angelo thought to himself.

He landed in front of the graves and, without consciously meaning to, waved of his hand in front of them. Seconds later, the flowers were consumed by white flames and burned away.

"It can't be," Angelo said.

On each grave, the surname "EDWARDS" was engraved in large letters. Angelo squatted to read the smaller first names engraved above the "EDWARDS" on each tombstone, but was interrupted by the sound of a man clearing his throat from behind him.

"How terrible to know that you are going to kill everyone you ever loved or will love," the man said in a demonic voice. "Your wife…your kids…your entire world…reduced to sorrow and torment all because of their faith in a sorry excuse for a superhero."

Angelo quickly grabbed the handle of his sword, but before he could take it out, the demon, dressed in a black suit and wearing a multi-colored tie, was sitting on a tombstone at the end of the row, smiling at Angelo.

"No need to take that thing out," the demon said. "Even if it was actually there."

Angelo realized there was nothing in his hands and that his sword and sheath were gone.

"What's going on?" Angelo asked as his belt disappeared. "Who are you…and where are we? Are you warping reality or something?"

The demon tilted its head. "Why do you ask?"

"Because this is my greatest fear, becoming the Demon Master, and these are images that the Demon Master has placed in my head before, not something I have actually experienced. So, where are we?"

The demon applauded as he jumped off the tombstone and walked toward Angelo.

"You, my friend are very perceptive," the demon said. "I've never encountered anyone, and I do mean anyone, who has seen right through my 'Dread Reality' without me informing them of where they were just before I killed them."

"Well, I'm not just anyone," Angelo said as he tightened his fists. "Who are you?"

"My name is Fear and I'm going to…"

"Kill me with my fear?" Angelo asked. "I hope you don't say that to all of your victims because it's pathetic."

Fear shook his fist and bared his teeth as he transformed into a seven-foot tall, red, hairy beast with large orange eyes and razor claws.

"HOW DARE YOU INSULT THE MASTER OF FEAR?" Fear screamed as he swiped at Angelo.

Angelo continued tightening his fists and swung at Fear as if he had his sword and shield in his hands.

Fear, still in beast form, stood back. At first, it appeared he was shocked. But a few seconds later, he began to laugh.

"What do you think you are doing, boy?"

"Fighting back," Angelo said as his sword and shield appeared in his hands. His belt reappeared seconds later. "There's no way you could make my weapons disappear unless we were in my mind or you were affecting my mind. Either way, you are not the master of it. I am."

"That's not possible," Fear said as his bestial form increased in size and height. "I control what happens in this reality."

"This is *my* mind, not yours," Angelo said after tapping a button on his earpiece. "Besides, I knew this wasn't true when you mentioned my wife and kids, which I haven't had yet. One of the drawbacks from not having complete control of your victims, huh? You're not really here in my head, are you?"

Fear pounded on the ground and the Dread Reality became dark and stormy.

"If I kill you here," Fear said, "you'll die out there. It doesn't matter where I really am."

Angelo grinned as he touched his earpiece. "Angeline? I'm not sure you can hear me, but there's something I need to tell you. Listen carefully."

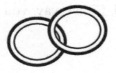

Angeline stood up and her sais appeared in her hands as she ran toward Fear.

"Angeline," Angelo said through her earpiece, "if you are currently seeing your worst fear, it's not real. A demon called Fear is causing us to see the thing we fear the most. It's not real...do you hear me, Angeline?"

"Loud and clear," Angeline said as she touched her ear. Even though her earpiece appeared to be gone, she knew in reality it was still there.

"What's loud and clear?" Fear said as he took a step back.

"The fact that you are trying to trick me," Angeline said as she ran toward Fear. "My partner, who you just threatened to kill, just informed me he is fighting you in his mind and that I must be doing the same."

"That's impossible," Fear said. "He could only tell you that if your minds were linked. But, even if they are, you'll both be dead soon. As long as I'm in your minds, you two are in a catatonic state in the real world. Soon, hundreds of demons will feast on your flesh and your world will belong to my master."

Angeline kicked Fear in the head. "You bad guys never learn to keep your mouths shut. You would win if you didn't reveal your entire plan to the heroes."

Angeline reached for Fear but he quickly rolled away and disappeared.

Seconds later, Fear reappeared, with 10 duplicates of himself.

"I've killed countless souls by showing them their greatest fears and I'm not about to be stopped by some little girl and her sunglasses-wearing boyfriend," Fear said. "I am the master of fear and horror."

"Actually," a male voice said from behind the line of Fears, "you're about to become dust."

Four of the duplicates disappeared as a shining sword sliced through their torsos. As the duplicates disintegrated, Angelo could be seen standing where they had been.

"Impossible," Fear said to Angelo. "You can't be here."

"Nothing's impossible," Angeline said as she threw her sais into two duplicates. "Haven't you learned that by now?"

"Oh, I know that," Fear said. "That's why this… is possible."

The sky turned black and Angeline, Angelo and Fear appeared to be in a void. Even though everything around them was dark, the three could see each other.

"Since you invited yourself to Angeline's mind, Angelo, I'm going to invite some of your loved ones here," Fear said.

Fear snapped his fingers and Kevin's mother, father and sister appeared. Each was being held by a duplicate of Fear.

The duplicates forced the Edwardses to kneel down. Swords appeared in the hands of the duplicates, who had each placed their right foot on the back of one of their hostages, ready to strike.

"Now, unless you two give me your rings and renounce your powers," Fear said, "I will kill Angelo's family one by one before your eyes."

"Angelo, it isn't real," Angeline said. "They are not really here."

"I am," Angelo said. "If I am, then they could be to."

"But…"

"I can't take a risk on losing one of them," Angelo said as he slipped off his ring. "Fear, here is my ring. I renounce my power. Please let my family go."

Fear smiled. "Good boy. I'm glad you've seen things my way. But, the deal is that you both do it."

Angelo turned to Angeline. "Angeline, give me your ring."

"This is not right, Kevin," Angeline whispered. "There's no guarantee that he will let us and your family go after he gets what he wants."

"I don't care," Angelo said. "I can't gamble with their lives and I won't let you gamble with them either."

"What are you saying?"

Angelo looked at Fear and Fear nodded. A gleeful smile appeared on Fear's face as his eyes turned orange and he handed Angelo his ring, which was now black and glowing red, back to him.

"I'm saying I will do whatever it takes to save my family," Angelo said as he put his ring back on. His aura turned from white to red and his eyes glowed red from behind his shades. "Even if that means killing you to do it."

"Angeline, come in," Angelo said as he continued to touch his earpiece. "I heard you say 'loud and clear,' but I couldn't make out what you said after that."

Fear laughed. "I couldn't let the two of you team up against me. So, as soon as you sent that first message, I jammed the frequency. No more phoning home."

Angelo pulled the hilt of his sword apart, forming two swords. "Fine. Let's go."

"Oh, you won't be fighting me," Fear said. "My darlings will be your combatants."

"Who?"

Two armed young women appeared behind Angelo. He nearly dropped his weapons when he saw who Fear's "darlings" were.

There stood Angeline, glowing red, with her sais drawn, and a zombified version of Melanie, armed with an automatic crossbow.

"Ladies, do whatever you need to do to get that ring," Fear said. "I don't care if he is alive or dead when you finish, just get me that ring."

"Yes, master," Angeline and Melanie said as they bowed to Fear.

"Wake up," Wiseman J said as he shook Angelo. "Come on. We need you."

Jeff stood a couple of feet away, fighting a group of advancing demons, all eager to rip apart and devour the catatonic Angelo he was trying to protect.

"J, you have got to get him up and soon," Jeff said. "My arms are getting really tired."

"I'm trying, Jeff, but he isn't responding."

"Any sign of Angeline?" Jeff asked as the last demons he had been fighting burst into flames and burned into ashes.

"None," Wiseman J said. "I've been trying to reach her since we saw that explosion, but she isn't answering."

Jeff sat down and tried to catch his breath. "Well, we need to get Angelo out of the open. He's a sitting duck for every demon that runs or flies by."

A dozen demons ran from around the corner of a nearby building and spotted Jeff, Wiseman J and Angelo.

"You're right," Wiseman J said. "But, it's too late to move Angelo."

Jeff stood up and twirled his staff. "So, here's the plan, J. You go look for Angeline and I'll stay here and do my best to protect Angelo."

"Are you sure?" Wiseman J asked.

"Yeah," Jeff said. "I should be okay until you get back."

"Okay," Wiseman J said as he stood up and ran in the direction that he had seen Angeline fighting Destruction. "I'll be back as soon as possible."

"Man," Jeff said as he fought a new group of demons. "I'm starting to regret going through that portal. I guess this is how Kevin and Juanita felt when they came to our world."

"Angelo, you have to stop this," Angeline said as she dodged Angelo's attacks. "We can defeat Fear together and save your family."

"No, there is no defeating Fear," Angelo said. "Give me your ring or I will have to take it from you."

"Angelo…Kevin," Angeline said as she flew above him. "I love you and I know you love me. Please don't do this."

The darkness of the void lifted and buildings, streets and the sky became visible.

"LOVE ME?!!!" Angelo screamed as he threw Angeline through a building. "HOW CAN YOU LOVE ME? YOU LEFT ME, ALONE AND WITHOUT AN EXPLANATION!"

Angeline climbed out of the rubble of a wall that had collapsed on top of her and found Angelo standing over her. He lifted her up into the air by her throat with his left hand and pulled out his sword with his right hand.

"Kevin…please don't," Angeline said, her voice barely audible as Angelo tightened his grip.

"I remember making the same plea to you as you broke my heart," Angelo said as his eyes grew redder. "I begged you not to leave me, promised to make whatever was wrong better and you still abandoned me."

"You're right," Angeline said. "I...I...was afraid."

Angelo's grip lessened and he lowered his sword. "Of what?"

"Of not loving you as much as you loved me and hurting you like Carmen did," Angeline said. "And look what I did...I let my fear get the best of me and I did exactly what I didn't want to do."

"NOOOOOO," Fear screamed. "DON'T LISTEN TO HER. SHE'S LYING!"

"No, I'm not, Kevin," Angeline said as she turned into Juanita and Angelo let her go. "I love you and if I could do it all over, I would never have left you."

"You promise?" Angelo said as his eyes turned from red back to normal.

"I do," Juanita said as she leaned in and kissed Angelo on the lips. "I love you and I'm never going to hurt you or leave you again."

Angelo, with a smile on his face, faded away, as did his family and the duplicates of Fear.

Fear backed away as Juanita transformed into Angeline and walked toward him.

"Look, Sweetheart," Fear said as he stumbled backwards and fell to the ground. "I was just doing what I was commanded to do. Do you think I like making people live out their worst fears?"

"Yes," Angeline said as she stood over Fear.

"Well, I don't," Fear said. "Fear isn't even my real name. It's Douglass."

"I don't care," Angeline said as she pulled out a sai.

"Wait," Fear said. "You defeated your fear. Congratulations. You're the first one to break out of my Dread Reality. You passed the test."

"You're right," Angeline said. "Now you know what you can do?"

"Yes?"

"GET OUT OF MY MIND," Angeline said as she stabbed Fear in the heart.

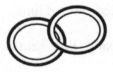

"This is not real," Angelo said as Angeline's sais clanged against his shield.

"Oh, it's real," Zombie Melanie said as she fired several rounds of poison arrows at Angelo from her automatic crossbow. "Soon, you'll join me as a member of the undead."

"Oh, not until I pull his heart out and break it into tiny pieces like I did when I broke up with him," Angeline said.

Angelo flew high into the air to get away, but Angeline was close behind.

"You really think you can run away from me?" Angeline asked. "I'm the one who runs away. Not you. You're the monster. You're the one that no one could ever truly love."

Angelo stopped and let Angeline catch up to him.

"How can you say that?" Angelo asked.

"Look at you," Angeline said. "You are nothing but a fat, lonely little boy playing dress up. You're no hero. Now, Jeff, that's a hero and a real man."

Angelo balled up his fist.

"So, are you going to hit me now?" Angeline asked.

"I…can't and I won't," Angelo said.

"Good," Angeline said as her eyes grew redder and she sucker punched Angelo. "Because I can and will hit you."

Angelo crashed into the street below, creating a giant crater. A few second later, Zombie Melanie shot poison arrows at him.

"Welcome back to earth, failure," she said.

"I'm not a failure," Angelo as his shield appeared in his hand.

"Oh, really? Then why am I dead? I thought you loved me?"

"Oh, didn't you know, Melanie," Angeline said as she landed, "that he has a habit of letting down the women he claims to love?"

"That's not true," Angelo said as he stood up. "I did everything I could to save you, Melanie. Everything. It felt like I was knocking on death's door when I was fighting that demon, which turned out to be the Demon

Master. I pushed past the hurt, the blood loss and the loss of consciousness to fight for you."

"You did?" Zombie Melanie asked as she stopped firing the arrows.

"I did," Angelo said. "I might not have loved you like I love Juanita, but I was still willing to die to save your life and I regret every day that I didn't save you. But, I'm no longer afraid that I didn't do all I could because I did."

With those words, Zombie Melanie transformed into an alive Melanie, who smiled and faded away.

"Kill him now, Angeline," Fear said. "Do not listen to his lies."

"Yes, master," Angeline said, pulling out her bow and arrow.

"Angie…Nita, I love you and I also know that I did abandon you when you needed my help the most," Angelo said. "And if you had died while I was off sulking, I would never have forgiven myself. I was so afraid that something would happen to you that I ended up becoming that something when I fought Despair and Despond."

"SHUT UP!" Angeline screamed as she aimed for Angelo's heart.

Angelo dropped his shield and walked toward Angeline so she could have a better shot.

"It's okay, Nita," he said. "I know that I made a lot of mistakes when it came to us. I was always afraid that I was going to lose you and in having that fear, I might have driven you away. But, I'm not afraid anymore. I'm not afraid anymore that we will never get back together. If we are nothing more than friends for the remainder of our lives, I will be the best friend I can be and I will always love you, no matter what, from one world to the next."

Angeline dropped her bow and arrow and faded away.

"NOOOOOOO!" Fear screamed. "This is not over."

"Yes, it is, Fear," Angelo said as he threw his sword toward Fear.

The sword flew into Fear's chest and he screamed in agony as he burst into flames.

"Now, get out of my head," Angelo said.

"Are you okay, Angeline?"

Angeline opened her eyes and saw Wiseman J kneeling down beside her.

"Yes," she said. "I think so. Where is Fear?"

Wiseman J looked around. "Who is 'Fear'?"

"I was trapped inside my mind by a demon who was using my fears to try to get me to give up my powers."

"I didn't see any demon when I got here," Wiseman J said. "All I saw were the people who you saved. The law enforcement officers have been fighting demons that have tried to come near you."

Angeline smiled as Wiseman J helped her to stand. "Where's Angelo and Jeff?"

"Jeff is guarding Angelo. He's in a state much like you were."

"We need to get to him as soon as possible," Angeline said looking at the battle between the demons and the law enforcement officers. "But, first, I need to end this fight. Go get some wheels, Wiseman J and meet me back here in a few minutes. Contact Jeff and let him know we'll be there soon."

Jeff collapsed and sighed as he let go of his staff after defeating a group of 50 demons. He looked over at Angelo and hit the ground.

"WAKE UP," Jeff screamed. "As much as I hate to admit it, I really need YOUR HELP!"

The rubble under Angelo moved as he moaned and regained consciousness.

"What's going on?" Angelo asked as he sat up.

"Your world is falling apart and I've been fighting to protect your sorry…"

Static and feedback from his earpiece stopped Jeff from finishing his sentence.

"Jeff, this is J. I found Angeline. As soon as she is finished defeating some demons, we'll be there to help you with Angelo."

"No rush, J," Jeff said as he watched Angelo stand up. "'The demon slayer' has awakened and appears to have completely healed."

"That's great news," Wiseman J said. "We'll be there as soon as Angeline wraps things up."

"Okay, J," Jeff said. "Be careful."

Jeff looked at Angelo like he smelled something that had rotted.

"What's wrong?" Angelo asked after catching the glance.

"Nothing but the fact that you are a pathetic excuse for a hero," Jeff said as his eyes glowed bright green.

"Excuse me," Angelo said.

"No," Jeff said as he jabbed an end of his staff into Angelo's chest. "No more excuses for you. Why don't you just lie back down on the ground and get yourself some shut eye, princess?"

Angelo's eyes glowed bright green also as he swatted the staff away. "You better back off."

"Or what, you're gonna hit me again?"

"Maybe I should have broken your jaw on Dark Earth so I wouldn't have to hear you jabber on like an idiot right now."

"Go ahead and try it," Jeff said as he twirled his staff and circled Angelo. "There's only going to be one 'demon slayer' soon and it's going to be me."

9

Green-Eyed Monsters

Angelo pulled his sword out with his right hand as his shield appeared in his left hand.

"That's right, Angelo," Jeff said as his eyes continued to glow green. "Pull out your fancy weapons and powers to fight a man who has no powers."

"It's not my fault you weren't chosen to protect your own world," Angelo said as his aura turned green. "Even God knows you're not man enough to be a leader on your world. That's why Angeline and I had to save it."

Neither Jeff or Angelo noticed the smiling green-eyed demoness, who watched from the ledge of a nearby building, as the two heroes insulted, taunted and ridiculed each other.

Jeff opened his mouth, revealing large, growing fangs. "I've been saving your butt since you first arrived on my planet. I saved you from those demon dogs at my world's library and then had to come here, today, to your world, to save you, once again from demons at a library, in the same exact way."

"Well, at least I didn't allow myself to get captured by a demoness and become her giant, furry pet and slave," Angelo said.

"Really?" Jeff asked. "I'd gladly be a monster than be a jerk and a coward like you. At least I didn't let Melanie get taken."

Angelo's eyes flashed red and then turned green again as he lunged at Jeff.

Jeff dodged Angelo's attack and his staff turned green as he slammed it into Angelo.

Angelo was knocked into the air and crashed into a car down the street.

The demoness laughed and clapped as she watched the mayhem she was causing. "Let's turn it up a notch, shall we?" she asked the green-eyed monsters who sat next to her.

Angelo's aura turned green and so did his weapons and clothes. "You're going to pay for that."

Before Angelo could get off the car, it exploded as an invisible force pounded down on it.

The force was one of the demoness' green-eyed monsters, which like her, was invisible. It backed away from Angelo and waited for its master's next command.

"I don't know how you did that," Angelo said walking out of the explosion, "but it's time I rid both of our worlds of your presence."

Angelo flew at super speed toward Jeff, who jumped out of the way just in time to keep from being killed by the impact.

The winds created by Angelo's super speed attack tossed Jeff through the glass doors of a building.

Angelo landed in front of the building. "Come out, Jeff. Come to the demon slayer."

Angelo waited for Jeff to say something as the sounds of growls grew from within the building.

"Great," Angelo said. "Demons dogs got to him before I could. At least I don't have to hear his whiny voice anymore."

My voice…isn't whiny, said a growling voice from within Kevin's head.

Large green eyes peered out at Angelo as the ground shook. Large, dark green paws shot out of the building and struck Angelo. The paws were followed by long hairy black arms with a green tint, then a large black werewolf head. Large, dark green wings flapped, and burst through the walls of the building.

"Monstrosity," Angelo said as he flew to face the creature. "Looks like you're half the monster you once were."

I might be smaller, but I'm still stronger and smarter than you, Monstrosity said telepathically.

"Now that's a twist I didn't see coming," the green-eyed demoness said as she jumped down to the street.

"I'm putting you down like I did before," Angelo said as he uppercutted Monstrosity.

The blow caused Monstrosity to stumble backwards and into the building he had transformed in. As Monstrosity hit the ground, the building caved in on him.

Angelo smiled and turned away. "That's that."

You wish, coward, Monstrosity said as he rose from the rubble. *I'm not that easy to get…That's odd.*

"What's odd, monster?" Angelo asked, ready to strike Monstrosity again.

Monstrosity took several long sniffs and turned his nose toward the demoness and her green-eyed monsters.

Someone is watching us fight and I can smell her powers all over us, Monstrosity told Angelo. *She is trying to control us and I don't let anyone control me.*

"Right," Angelo said. "Stop stalling, hairy."

See for yourself, Monstrosity said as he linked Angelo's mind with his so Angelo could see through his eyes.

Through Monstrosity's eyes and super vision, Angelo could see the green-eyed demoness and her green-eyed monsters.

"Who are you?" Angelo asked as he broke the link with Monstrosity and unsheathed his sword. "You can stop hiding now. We know you're there."

The green-eyed demoness and her green-eyed monsters shimmered into plain slight a few seconds later.

"Well, I guess our fun is over," the green-eyed demoness said to her green-eyed monsters. "Kill them."

She was controlling us, Monstrosity told Angelo telepathically.

"Duh," Angelo said as he fought four of the green-eyed monsters.

Listen to me, Monstrosity said. *She's using our jealously of each other against us. We have to...*

"I'm not jealous of you," Angelo said as he threw a green-eyed monster into the ground. "Never, ever will I be jealous of a weakling like you. I have so much power and I'm so much better than you."

Angelo's aura turned from green to red after he spoke those words and he impaled the green-eyed monsters around him.

Monstrosity flapped his wings and ascended high into the sky. His mind became clearer and clearer as he distanced himself from the green-eyed demoness. The color of his entire body returned to normal as the jealousy and rage he had felt moments before faded away.

Ahhh, that's better, Monstrosity thought as he soared in the sky. *Now to get Angelo up here before he destroys the city and everyone in it.*

Monstrosity's massive red chest expanded as he took a deep breath, stopped flapping his wings and plummeted to earth like a bomb being dropped from a plane.

The sound of Monstrosity's descent stopped all who were fighting, screaming, killing and running in the chaotic city. Demons and humans all looked up in wonder and awe as a large, flaming object fell from the sky.

The green-eyed demoness ran as Monstrosity crashed through the street and spread open his wings, instantly putting out the flames that had covered his body and igniting all of the green-eyed monsters surrounding him.

"I don't need your help," Angelo said as his aura grew redder and redder. "Go back where you came from before I personally send you there."

THAT'S ENOUGH, Monstrosity said as he used his snout to toss Angelo several feet into the air. Monstrosity flew behind Angelo and once again, with his snout, pushed Angelo higher into the sky.

"STOP IT," Angelo said, trying to push Monstrosity back to earth. "DO YOU WANT ME TO KILL YOU?!!!"

Angelo pulled out his sword as he and Monstrosity neared the invisible barrier around Memphis.

"So be it," Angelo said as he prepared to strike Monstrosity down.

Monstrosity backed away and suddenly Angelo's aura turned from red to green to white.

Angelo holstered his sword and shook his head. He looked over at Monstrosity.

"Jeff, I'm sorry," Angelo said. "I lost it really bad there for a few minutes. I was going to kill you."

It's okay, Monstrosity said. *I would have probably tried to do the same thing if I hadn't had anger management.*

Angelo paused for a few seconds and then pulled out his sword.

What's wrong, Angelo? Monstrosity asked.

"Monstrosity is supposed to be gone, so why am I talking to him…a much smaller, but still terrifying version of him?"

It's a long story and too long to tell while the Demon Master and his army are destroying your city, Monstrosity said. *But trust me, I, Jeff, am in control...at least for now. We need to get back down there and I need you to get my duffel bag and inject two syringes into me.*

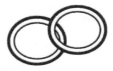

Angeline, with Wiseman J in her arms, touched down next to Angelo and looked around as she put Wiseman J down.

"Are you okay?" she asked Angelo.

"Yeah. Are you?"

"Yeah," she said. "What happened here? We saw that giant ball of fire come down and crash here. I could have sworn I saw giant wings."

"It's a long story," Angelo said. "Did you happen to see a green-eyed demoness on your way here?"

"No, we didn't," Angeline said. "They have green eyes now? When did that happen?"

Angelo hunched. "I don't know, but if you didn't see her, then she's gone."

"Where's Jeff?" Wiseman J asked.

"Right here," Jeff said as he walked toward them. He was tucking in an orange tank top and putting on a belt over some faded black jeans.

"What happened to your fatigues?" Angeline asked.

"Again, it's a long story," Angelo said, "and right now, we don't have time to really go into it. We need to end this now."

"Agreed," Wiseman J said. "But, we don't know where the Demon Master is."

"Well, we've fought three of his lieutenants," Angelo said.

"Well, technically, we didn't fight the green-eyed demoness," Jeff said. "She ran away before we could get to her."

"So, that means we have Belicista and two demonesses to take out," Angeline said.

"Well, you can put Belicista down as the next demon we have to fight," Wiseman J said as he pointed to a flat-screen television playing in the damaged lobby of the building he stood in front of.

Onscreen, a news reporter pointed down Main Street toward 100 North Main, the tallest building in Memphis, standing at 430 feet with 37 stories.

The camera focused in on Belicista leading an army of elite demon soldiers down the street, killing everyone in their sights. The camera tilted and showed demons crawling up 100 North Main, toward screaming people on the rooftop.

"If anyone knows where The Demon Master is, it's Belicista," Wiseman J said. "We need to get him to tell us where he is."

"Plus, I have a score to settle with him," Jeff said.

"That'll come later," Wiseman J said. "First, we save those people and then we deal with Belicista."

Tyrone Tony Reed Jr.

10

A Score to Settle

Angeline and Angelo, who carried Jeff, used their super speed to arrive near 100 North Main in three seconds.

"Here's the plan," Angelo said.

Jeff held up his hand. "Wiseman J is back there retrofitting an SUV with purity bombs, which illuminate, creating purity lights that destroy demons. Since he's not here, we are going to do things our way. And when I say our way, I mean my way."

Angelo and Angeline looked at each other, back at Jeff and nodded.

"Angeline, you're going to fly me up to the top of Kent Tower and I'm going to taunt Belicista to meet me on the 18th floor," Jeff said. "While I'm making my way down from the top, Angeline will rescue the people on the rooftop and follow behind me after she is finished. Angelo, you'll come up from behind Belicista's army and start picking them off."

"So, I'll be behind Belicista when he gets to the 18th floor and it'll just be the three of us and Belicista?" Angelo asked.

"Exactly," Jeff said.

Angelo gave Jeff the thumbs up. "Sounds like a solid plan," Angelo said as he flew off the ground. "See you two on the 18th floor."

Angelo flew higher and shot past Belicista and his elite army.

Belicista raised his battle-axe and his army paused.

"SEE HOW THE STUPID HEROES RUN?" Belicista asked. "BEFORE THE END OF THIS DAY,

WE WILL RULE THIS CITY AND THEN THIS WORLD!"

The demon soldiers raised their weapons and cheered.

"That's our cue," Jeff said to Angeline as he strapped his duffel bag to his back.

Angeline grabbed Jeff by the arms and flew him to the top of 100 North Main.

A group of 20 people, with startled expressions, backed away in fear as Jeff jumped down onto the rooftop and Angeline landed beside him.

"STAY BACK," one of the men in the group said.

"It's okay," Angeline told them. "I'm here to get you down and away from here."

"Listen to her and do what she says," Jeff said. "She's here to help."

Angeline smiled at Jeff. "Don't you have a demon lieutenant to taunt?"

"I do."

"Be careful," Angeline said as she created a force field around the group of people. "I'll be right back and won't be too far behind you."

Angeline flew off the rooftop, followed by the force field full of people, and flew away.

"Here goes nothing," Jeff said as he walked to the edge of the roof. He looked down and spotted Belicista and his army a few feet away from the entrance of the building.

In the distance, Jeff could see a blur of movement at the rear of the advancing army. The demon soldiers were being destroyed by a fast moving white and blue figure.

That's it, Angelo, Jeff said.

Jeff reached into his pockets and threw several purity bombs down in front of Belicista.

Belicista stopped and his army followed suit. He looked up at Jeff and growled.

"HEY, UGLY," Jeff screamed. "IT'S BEEN A WHILE. I THOUGHT YOU WERE DEAD. WHY DON'T YOU MEET ME ON THE 18TH FLOOR SO WE CAN END THIS FEUD?"

Belicista threw his battle-axe up toward Jeff and drummed on his breastplate as the battle-axe soared through the sky.

The battle-axe struck the rooftop, missing Jeff by a few inches.

"ALMOST, BUT NOT QUITE," Jeff screamed. "SEE YOU SOON!"

Jeff opened the rooftop access door and headed down a flight of stairs as a flying demon soldier reached the rooftop.

The demon soldier pulled the battle-axe out of the rooftop and tossed it down to Belicista. The demon soldier was soon joined by 10 more flying demon soldiers on the rooftop and they all headed down the stairs after Jeff.

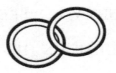

Angelo had made it halfway through Belicista's army when he saw Belicista catch his battle-axe and run through the glass entrance doors of 100 North Main.

"He's taking the bait," Angelo said into his earpiece.

"I had no doubt," Jeff said. "Only thing I didn't know was that there were already demon soldiers inside. I'm taking them out as I go."

"I'll be there soon," Angeline said. "I'm dropping these people off at a military checkpoint and I'll be headed back there in a few minutes."

"Okay," Angelo said. "Jeff, I know how important this is for you. So, I want you to know that you can do this. After seven years…"

"Eight," Jeff said before he realized what he had said.

"What?" Angelo asked.

"Nothing," Jeff said.

"I just wanted to let you know that I believe you can do this," Angelo said. "You don't need powers to be a hero because you're already one."

"Thanks, Angelo," Jeff said. "I appreciate you saying that."

A high-pitched sound and static followed Jeff's words.

"Jeff, are you still there?" Angelo asked. "Jeff?"

Jeff's earpiece fell to the floor as he struggled against two demon soldiers in the stairwell of the 22nd floor.

A third demon soldier stepped on the earpiece, smashing it as it made its way to help the other two demon soldiers.

Jeff pushed his way to a wall and ran up it, making the demon soldiers let him go. He landed on the third demon soldier, picked up his staff and impaled the two demon soldiers who had been holding him.

The demon soldiers burst into flames, while the third demon soldier grabbed Jeff's staff, yanking it away. The demon soldier's hands burst into flames, followed by the rest of its body, but it continued to hold on to Jeff's staff.

"What in the world?" Jeff asked as the demon soldier laughed.

Suddenly, the door to the 22nd floor opened and several more demon soldiers entered the stairwell.

"Great," Jeff said. "These things are getting even smarter."

"Don't worry," a female voice said from the floor above. "I got them."

Ten purity arrows flew down from the 23rd floor and went through the heads of the ten demon soldiers, causing them to burst into flames. The demon soldier holding Jeff's staff finally let it go as it burned into ashes.

A few seconds later, Angeline walked down a set of stairs to Jeff, who was surrounded by 11 piles of ashes."

"Thanks," Jeff said.

"Anytime," Angeline said as her bow disappeared.

The doors of the 21st and 20th floors opened and more demon soldiers poured into the stairwell.

Jeff picked up his staff as Angeline pulled out her sais and together, they attacked the demon soldiers.

"GO," Angeline shouted to Jeff. "I've got this."

"Are you sure?" Jeff asked.

Angeline tossed both of her sais into the air and the sais flew through all of the demon soldiers in the stairwell.

"I guess that's a 'yes,'" Jeff said as Angeline smiled and waved him away.

More doors flew open on the floors above them as Angeline's sais returned to her. She touched her earpiece as she walked toward Jeff.

"What is it?" Jeff asked.

"Angelo said Belicista is on the 15th floor," Angeline said. "You don't want him to beat you to the 18th floor do you?"

"Just two more floors to go," Jeff said as he ran down the stairs.

"We'll meet you there," Angeline said.

Two minutes later, Jeff stood in the center of the 18th floor, cracking his neck and bouncing around like a boxer as he twirled his glowing staff in the open office space.

Jeff heard the stairwell door open and immediately paused. *This is it,* he thought to himself. *Well, I did think the same thing two years ago...*

Jeff watched as Belicista rammed through the doorframe and walked toward him.

"ARE YOU READY?" Belicista asked as his gruff voice echoed across the floor and bounced off the windows and walls.

"I've been ready," Jeff said as he started the fight by throwing purity bombs in Belicista's face.

Belicista laughed as he swatted the bombs away and took out his battle-axe. "Nice try. My turn."

As Belicista swiped at Jeff's head, Jeff leapt backwards and hit him in the helmet with his staff.

Belicista grabbed the staff, singeing his hand, and tossed it and Jeff into a nearby pillar.

Two quick gusts of wind made Belicista look back toward the stairwell. When he turned back to face Jeff, he saw Angelo and Angeline helping him up.

"NEVER HEARD OF A FAIR FIGHT?" Belicista asked.

"Sure we have," Angeline said.

"We're just here to make sure it is fair and that it stays that way," Angelo said.

"ALLOW ME TO ASSIST," Belicista said as he pulled out a ram's horn and blew into it.

Angelo and Angeline took out their weapons as elite demon soldiers stormed out of the stairwell and into the office space.

"We'll handle them, Jeff," Angelo said as he and Angeline ran past Belicista and toward the demon soldiers. "You take care of Belicista. But don't kill him."

Belicista laughed again. "HE… KILL ME? IMPROBABLE AND IMPOSSIBLE."

"Maybe with all that armor you are hiding behind," Angeline said as she took out three demon soldiers. She ran behind Belicista at super speed and tore off his back plate and chest plate.

Angelo destroyed two demon soldiers and yanked off Belicista's helmet.

Together, Angelo and Angeline ripped off the armor on Belicista's arms, hands and legs.

"There," Angeline said as she and Angelo went back to fighting the demon soldiers. "That should make things fair."

"Thanks guys," Jeff said as he slammed his staff across Belicista's red, bare chest.

The crystal on the end of the staff glowed very brightly as it tore into Belicista's chest. Belicista grabbed his chest as blood streamed from his wound.

"Been a long time since you were hurt like that, huh?" Jeff asked.

Belicista snarled at Jeff and charged toward him. He swung his battle-axe wildly, missing Jeff each time as he handicapped himself by continuing to clutch his bleeding wound.

"You've had this coming for some time now," Jeff said. "All of the people you and your kind murdered, it's time for you all to pay."

Jeff ran toward Belicista, slid between his legs and jabbed his staff into the back of Belicista's knees.

The 400-pound red demon dropped onto his knees and screamed so loudly that the demon soldiers all stopped in their tracks.

The demon soldiers ran toward their commander, but as they did, they were lifted into the air by Angeline's telekinesis.

"Where do you all think you're going?" Angeline asked as she made the force field shrink.

The demon soldiers pounded on the force field, but soon could not move at all.

Angeline waved her hand and a small hole opened up.

Angelo pulled out several purity bombs and tossed them into the hole and Angeline sealed the force field.

There were numerous flashes of light as the demon soldiers burst into flames and burned into ashes.

Belicista reached for his ram's horn again, but Jeff kicked it off his belt and slammed his staff into Belicista's neck. Jeff pinned Belicista, holding the staff against Belicista's right temple.

Smoke and white flames shot out from Belicista's right eye as he screamed.

Angelo and Angeline walked past Jeff and looked down on Belicista.

"Where is your master?" Angelo asked.

Belicista snapped at Angelo between his screams. "I…will…not…betray…him," he said, his words barely audible.

Jeff pulled down on his staff, running it from Belicista's right temple to the right side of his neck. When Jeff stopped, he pressed the staff into Belicista's neck, burning a hole into it.

"Tell us where he is," Jeff said as he pressed harder.

"I'd…rather…die," Belicista said as he tried to crack a smile.

"Fine," Angelo said. "We'll find him on our own. Jeff, he's all yours."

Jeff released Belicista and pushed the demon on his back.

Jeff raised his staff, like a spear, over Belicista's chest, aiming for the demon's heart.

"Suffer in hell," Jeff said.

All the windows on the floor exploded and the glass flew to the center of the room before Jeff could stab Belicista in the heart.

Angelo and Angeline held their hands out and their shields appeared and expanded to cover themselves and Jeff. Angeline surrounded them with a force field for extra protection.

Belicista snickered as he faded away.

"NOOOOO," Jeff screamed as he watched his hated foe disappear.

Violent winds rushed into the office space for a few seconds before subsiding.

Angeline dropped her force field and the three heroes stood up and looked around.

"I can't believe he got away," Jeff said as he turned over a desk. "I was this close to killing him…"

"It's okay," Angeline said. "We'll find him and then you can finish him."

"That's funny," a female voice said from outside the building, "because I'm planning to finish you now."

A demoness, clad in a dark blue outfit, with two medieval scourges attached to her belt, flew down into the office space and smiled. Her dark blue eyes shimmered as she ran her blue fingernails through her sleek, jet-black hair.

"Since I've heard that most of my master's lieutenants introduce themselves to you before they attempt to kill you," the demoness said. "I guess I should introduce myself, especially since I will be the one who finally kills you."

"We've heard that before," Angelo said. "And they've all failed."

"YOU, SHUT UP!" the demoness said as her head cocked to the side like the big hand on an old clock. "I'LL GET TO YOU SOON ENOUGH!"

Angelo stepped back and so did Angeline and Jeff.

"You know her?" Jeff asked.

"No," Angelo said. "At least, I don't think I do."

"Well, she's upset with you about something," Angeline said. "I know that tone in her voice because I've had it with you a few times myself, Angelo."

"As I was saying," the demoness said, "my name is Scourge and it's time for you all to pay for sinning against my master."

Scourge then pointed at Angelo. "But you, boy, I'm going to kill you very, very slowly. I'm going to torture you for what you did to my brother and sister, Despair and Despond!"

"Well, now it makes sense," Jeff said as he looked at

Angelo. "It's all your fault."

11

The Wages of Sin

"Come here, boy," Scourge said to Angelo as she pulled out her scourges. "Time for me to cut your flesh off and eat it."

"No thanks," Angelo said as he pulled out his sword.

Scourge whipped her weapons toward Angelo's sword and the cords of the scourges attached to it. She yanked her weapons back and Angelo's sword flew out of his hands and slid out across the floor and out the window.

Angelo ran after his sword, but Scourge used one of her scourges and whipped his back and pulled him back to her.

"Owwww," Angelo said as the metal-plated cords of the scourges tore into his back. He pulled away and bloody pieces of his skin tore off and fell to the ground with the cords.

Angelo attached his shield to his back and held his hand out toward his sword, beckoning it to fly to him.

"What are you doing?" Scourge asked as her scourges glowed green. "There's no way your sword is going to come back…"

Scourge leapt backwards as Angelo's sword tore through the floor underneath her and flew into Angelo's hand.

"Clever trick," Scourge said.

"Here's another," Jeff said as he slammed his staff into the back of Scourge's head.

"And one for the road," Angeline said as she rammed her right fist into Scourge's face as Scourge fell forward.

The impact of the punch sent Scourge flying across the office space and into a closet room on the other end of the floor.

"Are you okay?" Angeline asked Angelo as Jeff removed Angelo's shield.

"I…think…so," Angelo said as he tried to straighten up.

"Looks like you're already healing up," Jeff said as he watched several long scars disappear on Angelo's back. Angelo's shirt followed suit, with the rips in the fabric mending together instantaneously.

Angelo stood straight up as the pain subsided. "That's better. Now, let's finish her."

"FINISH ME?!!!" Scourge screamed as the cords of her scourges tore through the walls and door of the closet room.

Scourge's jet-black hair was disheveled and her teeth had become fangs as she floated like a ghost toward the three heroes.

"DIEEEEEEEEE!!!" Scourge screamed as she whipped her scourges around at them.

Angeline held her hands out, creating a force field and forcing the demoness back.

Scourge pounded relentlessly at the force field as Angeline caused it to surround her.

"YOU CAN'T STOP ME," Scourge screamed as she continued to pound on the force field. "I WILL GET FREE AND KILL YOU ALL!"

"Right…" Jeff said as he twirled his staff and pointed it toward Scourge. "Don't fret. Your master will be joining you in hell soon."

The force field squeezed Scourge into a fetal position. She closed her eyes and stopped moving.

"Ready," Angeline said as she looked over at Angelo.

"Yep," Angelo said as he pulled several purity bombs from the pouches of his belt and walked over to the force field.

Angeline caused a small hole to open in the force field and Angelo prepared to toss the purity bombs in.

As Angelo reached toward the opening, Scourge's left hand burst through and grabbed his wrist.

"OWWWWWW," Angelo screamed as Scourge broke his right wrist with her left hand and shattered Angeline's force field with a right hook.

Scourge swung Angelo into a concrete pillar and stared creepily at Angeline and Jeff.

"You…teamed up…on me," Scourge said between each deep breath she took. "Then…you…tried to…kill me…ME!"

The air around Scourge crackled with energy as her dark blue eyes turned red. She held her hands out toward Angeline and Jeff as her fingernails grew eight inches.

"Now…let's see…what you…do when…you're on…an even…playing field," Scourge said as she jabbed her fingernails into her eyes and pulled her face apart.

"What is she doing?" Jeff asked as he fought back the urge to vomit. A few seconds later, he turned around and vomited in a trash can.

Angeline was unable to reply because her jaw had dropped in disbelief.

Angelo crawled over to them and stood up, his right wrist now healed.

"Whatever she's doing, it's not to our advantage," Angelo said. "Look."

Instead of blood flowing from Scourge's self-inflicted wounds, black, tar-like goo oozed out and into two large piles on the ground beside her.

"Get ready, you two," Angelo said to Jeff and Angeline. "Here comes trouble."

Scourge's fingernails shrank back to normal as she pulled them out of her face. Her wounds closed and she smiled at the heroes as the piles of goo stretched into the forms of two women.

They wore similar clothing to Scourge's, but in different colors, and had different weapons.

"This is my sister Bane," Scourge said as she gestured to the woman on her right, who was dressed in dark red clothing and armed with sickles.

"And this is my sister Desolate," Scourge said gesturing to the woman on her left, who was dressed in amber-colored clothing and had chains, with hooks at the end, coming out of the palm of her hands.

"We, the sisters of Despair and Despond will have our revenge on those who killed our siblings," the three demonesses said in unison.

"I'll take the woman with the bow," Desolate said.

"The male who just threw up is mine," Bane said as she ran toward Jeff.

"Great, sisters," Scourge said. "Angelo, the one who murdered our sister and brother, will be killed by me."

"RUN!" Angelo screamed at Angeline and Jeff.

Angelo threw handfuls of purity bombs toward the three demonesses as Angeline and Jeff ran for the stairwell.

The demonesses screamed and bared their teeth as the purity bombs exploded against their bodies.

Angelo pulled out his Sword of Faith with his right hand as his shield appeared in his left hand. He floated to the doorway of the stairwell and readied himself for the demonesses' attacks.

"Oh, look, sisters," Scourge said as the last of the purity bombs dissipated. "The little boy is going to try to protect his whittle friends from us."

"Not try," Angelo said as he twirled his sword and clanged it against his shield. "I will."

The demonesses laughed and gripped their weapons as they approached Angelo.

"Little boy, you die…today," Scourge said as she attacked Angelo.

It appeared Angeline and Jeff would have no trouble as they made their way to the lobby via the stairwell. But once they got 10 floors down, they found trouble on the 8th floor.

A large group of elite demon soldiers from Belicista's army were running up the stairs.

"Angeline, I can't do this," Jeff said as he slumped down to the stairs. "This is the Village of Dodoma all over again."

Angeline patted Jeff on the shoulder. "I understand. You rest up. I'll handle them."

"You sure?" Jeff asked as he watched Angeline crack her knuckles and pull out her sais.

Angeline jabbed one demon soldier in the forehead and slammed another demon soldier into three other demon soldiers.

Jeff could see a hint of a smile on Angeline face.

That woman is so awesome, he thought.

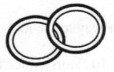

Angelo focused hard as he blocked the demonesses' various attacks with his sword and shield.

They moved at speeds that nearly made them invisible and Angelo willed himself to do the same.

That's it, Angelo, he thought to himself as he countered the demonesses' attacks. *You just need to buy Angeline and Jeff a few more minutes.*

Amber glowing chains with hooks shot out of Desolate's palms toward Angelo, who moved at just the right time for the hooks to sink into Bane's back.

"OWWWWWWW," Bane yelled as she gave her sister Desolate a look of disgust. "Watch where you are shooting those things."

"Sorry," Desolate said as she retracted her chains. "I didn't know he could move that fast."

"Actually, I can move faster," Angelo said as he sheathed his sword and made his shield disappear. He ran around Scourge, round-house kicked Desolate in the back of her head and raced up behind Bane.

Before Bane could move, Angelo had grabbed her sickles and thrown them toward Scourge and Desolate.

"How?" was the only word Bane could say as her sickles pierced Scourge's left arm and Desolate's right leg.

"It doesn't matter how he did it," Scourge said as she yanked Bane's sickle out of her arm and tossed it back to her. "Just make sure that he doesn't do it again."

When Scourge looked around the room, she saw Angelo standing in the doorway leading to the stairwell. She looked back at her sisters and gave them a displeased look. "I mean what I said. Don't let him do it again."

Angelo forced himself to grin, knowing that taunting the now bickering sisters would keep them off balance. "What do you say, ladies? Ready for round two?"

Jeff marveled at how fast Angeline moved as she took out her 60th elite demon soldier. Some of the demon soldiers had ran back down the stairs after seeing all of the ashes piled up on the stairwell.

Angeline had managed to clear four more floors, with only four more floors to go before she and Jeff reached the lobby.

"Have you reached J yet?" she asked Jeff as she threw a demon soldier through an office wall.

"Trying to contact him now," Jeff said as he pushed a button on his earpiece. "J, it's Jeff. We're almost at the lobby. We have four more floors to go. We'll probably be in the lobby in about…"

"Four minutes, six, tops," Angeline said as she used her telekinesis to push 20 demon soldiers down the stairs.

"That's good," Wiseman J said on the other side of the earpiece. "I'm almost done retrofitting the SUV with the purity bombs and two set of Christmas lights I found in a building."

"Well, we need you to be in the front of the building in less than six minutes," Jeff said.

"I'll do my best," Wiseman J said.

"I thought you said he was going to be easy to kill, Scourge?" Bane asked.

"He would be if you would stop complaining and catch him," Scourge said. "Keep this up and I'll be the one killing him while you're a pile of ashes on the floor."

"No chance," Angelo said as sweat flew from his face and the ground underneath his boots smoked and sizzled. He pushed himself to move so fast that he was able to see afterimages of himself.

"No way," the demonesses said in unison as they backed away. Angelo's speed had increased to the point that they could no longer see him.

Angelo attacked the demonesses, punching and kicking them to opposite areas of the office and preventing them from regaining their momentum.

Every few seconds, Angelo would slow down and as the fight persisted, his speed decreased.

"SEE THAT, SISTERS?" Scourged shouted. "THE BOY IS SLOWING DOWN!"

I've got to wrap this up before they kill me, Angelo thought. *But, I don't know if I can stop all three of them.*

Angelo slammed his shield into Bane and threw several purity bombs into Desolate's face. Both of the demonesses screamed as Angelo raced over to Scourge and tossed her into a pillar.

Scourge wobbled as she stood and tried to regain her bearings. "KILL HIM NOW!"

Bane threw several sickles at Angelo as Desolate's hooked chains shot out of the palm of her hands and chased Angelo around the office.

Angelo ducked and dodged the demonesses' weapons, which exploded through office furniture and pillars. He could hear the building creaking from the loss of several support beams as he raced around at super speed.

"Guys," Angelo said into his earpiece. "You need to get out of the building now. It's about to come down."

"We know," Jeff said into his earpiece. "We see cracks forming in the walls."

"We're in the lobby now," Angeline said.

A SUV came to a screeching halt in front of the glass doors of the building and the driver honked the horn.

"J is here, Angelo," Angeline said. "Come on down."

"Be there in a sec," Angelo said.

A group of demon soldiers stood in front of the lobby doors. They bared their teeth and readied their weapons before charging at Angeline and Jeff.

Angeline pushed her hands out toward the incoming demon soldiers and they fell backwards and were thrown through the glass doors and windows. They were instantly knocked unconscious by the force of Angeline's telekinesis.

"I'm so glad I'm not on your bad side anymore," Jeff said to Angeline as they ran out to the SUV.

"Where's Angelo?" Wiseman J asked as Jeff and Angeline got into the SUV.

"Up there, on the 18th floor, with three demonesses," Jeff said.

Angelo could barely catch his breath as the three demonesses continued to try to attack him with their weapons. His super speed had decreased and he had gotten weaker, which caused him to stumble or run into office furniture as he dodged the demonesses' attacks.

God, help me, Angelo said. *I can't keep this up.*

Angelo ducked before three of Bane's flying sickles could decapitate him. He was not, however, quick enough to avoid Desolate's hooked chains, which caught him around the ankles and slammed him into a nearby wall, which collapsed on him.

The demonesses high-fived each other as they walked to the rubble.

"See, sisters," Scourge said. "I told you it would be easy."

Angelo crawled out of the rubble and attempted to drag himself across the room. His legs had cramped up from running at super speed for so long.

"Look at the poor thing," Bane said, clicking her sickles together. "He's gone lame."

"Well, let's put him out of his misery," Desolate said as her hooked chains danced in the palm of her hands.

"No, sisters," Scourge said as she cracked her scourges. "He will suffer, for a very long time, for what he did to us and to Despair and Despond, our wickedly departed siblings."

Tears streamed down Angelo's face as the demonesses approached him. *God...please help me...I don't want to die like this.*

Angelo stopped moving and rolled onto his back when the demonesses caught up to him. *Please don't let me die like this.*

"Don't cry," Scourge said, noticing Angelo's tears. "You should save those tears for when the real pain begins."

The demonesses were about to laugh when a large, bright, white ball of light, shining from the other side of the building flew into the room and encased Angelo.

The ball of light burned the flesh of the demonesses and they flew for cover behind the remaining support beams of the floor.

"WHAT'S GOING ON?" Bane screamed at Scourge.

"I...DON'T KNOW," Scourge yelled back. "JUST STAY AWAY FROM IT!"

The ball of light whirled around Angelo and rose, with Angelo in the center of it. As it whirled, it got brighter and brighter and emitted energy similar to a giant purity bomb.

The demonesses screamed as the light shot out of the building.

The ball of light zipped out of the building and sped toward the SUV.

"What is that?" Jeff said as he pointed to the ball of light.

Angeline stood up in the sunroof and held her hands up toward the ball of light. "I don't know, but it's coming this way and I can't seem to stop it with my telekinesis."

Wiseman J tried to move the SUV, pressing the accelerator down hard. The wheels rolled so fast against the street that they smoked, but the SUV wouldn't budge.

Angeline placed a force field around the SUV, but the ball of light passed through it and stopped inside the SUV. A few seconds later, the light shot out of the

SUV, disintegrating nearby demon soldiers and clearing a path for the SUV.

When the light went out, Angelo was sitting next to Angeline in the back seat.

"That was awesome," Jeff said to Angelo. "But, next time, give us a heads up. Wiseman J almost peed his pants."

"I didn't do that," Angelo said. He turned and looked at Angeline. "I thought it was you."

"It wasn't," Angeline said.

"Well, let's chalk it up to that divine intervention I mentioned earlier and get out of here, because we've got company," Jeff said as the building collapsed and the three demonesses shot out of the falling debris.

Tyrone Tony Reed Jr.

12

Pain and Sorrow

The SUV sped through the streets of downtown Memphis, swerving around debris and abandoned vehicles.

"J, can't you go any faster?" Jeff asked.

"I'm trying," Wiseman J said as he made the SUV cut down an alley.

Jeff looked in the side view mirror and saw Scourge's disfigured face as she flew closer and closer to the SUV. "What happened to her?"

"That ball of light that brought me to you guys," Angelo said. "It was like a giant purity bomb."

"And neither one of you made it?" Wiseman J asked Angelo and Angeline.

"Nope," they said in unison.

"It's like I said...divine intervention," Jeff said."Someone is definitely looking out for us. We've had a lot of divine intervention today and now it looks like we can use a little bit more of it."

Angelo gave Jeff handfuls of purity bombs from the pouches on his belt, while Angeline created another force field around the SUV.

Jeff stood up in the sunroof and threw the purity bombs at the demonesses, while Angeline shot arrows at them from the back window on the passenger's side of the SUV.

"This just might work," Jeff said.

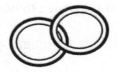

Bane flung sickle after sickle at the SUV but to no avail, as each sickle that hit Angeline's force field disintegrated upon impact.

"Desolate, do something," Bane said.

"I'm not shooting my chains at that thing," Desolate said. "If it destroyed your sickles, what do you think it'll do to the chains that are a part of me?"

"She's right," Scourge said as she flew beside her sisters. "You two distract the heroes."

"How?" Bane asked.

"You keep throwing your sickles at them," Scourge said. "Desolate, use your chains to throw cars, trucks and whatever else you fly by at them."

"What are you going to do?" Bane asked.

"You'll see," Scourge said as her eyes turned red and she flew high into the sky.

"She's cryptic as usual," Desolate said.

"Yes, but if it weren't for her, we wouldn't still exist," Bane said.

"Don't you go reminding me of that too," Desolate said. "Scourge does that enough already."

"Where's she going?" Jeff said as he watched Scourge fly so high and fast into the sky that he couldn't see her anymore.

"Wherever she's going, it can't be for anything good," Angelo said as he held his ribs. "But, I can say I'm glad to see her go."

"Which means we just need to get rid of these two demonesses," Angeline said as she continued to shoot arrows at Desolate and Bane.

"Yeah, which isn't easy when they keep throwing sickles and tossing cars at us," Wiseman J said as he swerved around the cars Desolate had thrown in front of the SUV.

"Guys, they're up to something," Angelo said as he thought about how fast the demonesses had moved when he had fought them earlier.

"What?" Jeff asked.

"They're quicker than this," Angelo said. "Just a few minutes ago, they were moving extremely fast and I would have been dead if that ball of light hadn't saved me."

"Which means?" Jeff asked.

"They are distracting us," Angeline said as she stopped firing her arrows and came back into the SUV.

Jeff followed suit. "From what?"

"HANG ON!" Wiseman J yelled as Scourge landed a few feet in front of the SUV.

Jeff fastened his seatbelt and Angeline did the same the SUV crashed into Scourge.

Scourge smiled as the SUV headlights burned the hairs off her skin and the front of the SUV collapsed in on itself. She used her left hand to lift the SUV and used its momentum to catapult the SUV into a tall building down the street.

The SUV, still surrounded by Angeline's force field, slammed through the top floors of the building and came to rest, upside down. The force field disappeared moments later.

The demonesses hovered several feet away from the gaping hole in the building and laughed.

"Great job, sister," Bane said.

"Show off," Desolate said, before giving Scourge a smile.

"Our siblings are finally avenged," Scourge said.

It took a couple of minutes for Wiseman J to regain consciousness and when he did, Angelo was unbuckling J's seatbelt so he could pull him out of the SUV.

Wiseman J saw Angeline crouching behind a set of desks and looking out of the hole in the building as Angelo pulled him from the vehicle.

"They're just hovering there," Angeline said as she watched Scourge, Bane and Desolate. "Looks like they're celebrating."

"That's good," Angelo said. "They probably think we're dead, which gives us the upper hand."

"How so?" Angeline said. "We're tired and they don't look like they've even broken a sweat."

"We have to make them break one and we can do that by separating them and hitting them fast and hard," Angelo said.

"So, what's the plan?" Jeff asked as he pulled out his staff and twirled it around.

"I'll take Scourge, especially since she's so focused on killing me," Angelo said. "I'm hoping that will make her overly arrogant and sloppy. Angeline, you take care of Desolate. Use her chains against her. Jeff, you should be able to take care of Bane and toss her sickles back at her with your staff."

"What about me?" Wiseman J asked. "Surely there's something for an old man to do."

"You're no old man, J," Angelo said. "And of course, there's something for you to do. Since you are so good with computers, use the ones in this office and find out what the news organizations and the law enforcement agencies have on the demon activity in the city. See if you can pinpoint where the Demon Master is."

"You're going to need a distraction to separate those demonesses," Wiseman J said.

"Oh, I've got the perfect distraction for them," Jeff said. "Follow me, guys."

"We're going to get started," Angeline said as she and Jeff walked over to the SUV.

"Angelo will be there in a moment," Wiseman J said as he motioned for Angelo to follow him to the office.

"What's up, J?" Angelo asked.

S.O.L.A.D.™: It's Just the Beginning

"I just wanted to let you know how proud I am of you three, especially you," Wiseman J said. "I can see, from your demeanor and the plans you have come up with, that you understand the gifts God has given you and the purpose He has created you for."

"I think I'm starting to," Angelo said. "I thought being a superhero was all fun and games, but I've learned that it's a serious and important job. After everything we've been through and everyone we've lost…"

"Melanie's death was not your fault," Wiseman J said as he watched Angeline use her telekinesis to turn the SUV right side up.

Angeline and Jeff pulled purity arrows from Angeline's quiver and piled them up inside the SUV. Every time they pulled a group of arrows out of the quiver, the quiver was replenished with more purity arrows.

"I know," Angelo said. "I just worry that we're going to lose more people we know here on my world. Try as we might, we can't save everyone."

"That's true," Wiseman J said. "But, you must never stop trying or evil will win."

"We're ready," Jeff said.

"That's my cue," Angelo said as he walked over to the SUV. He tossed handfuls of purity bombs through its windows .

When he was done, Angeline held her hands toward the SUV and used her telekinesis to smash the top of the SUV and seal the doors.

Angeline motioned for the SUV to rise from the floor, but Angelo gently lowered her hands.

"I've got this," Angelo said as he lifted the SUV over his head and walked to the hole. "Get your arrow ready. We need to get this done fast."

Angeline's bow appeared in her hand as she placed an arrow on the line and aimed it at the SUV's gas tank.

Angelo threw the SUV like a fastball out of the building and it slammed into Scourge. A second later, Angeline's arrow tore through the SUV's gas tank and the SUV exploded.

Purity arrows zipped through the air, striking the demonesses in several parts of their bodies. The purity bombs exploded on contact with the demonesses and they let out terrifying shrieks.

"NOW," Angelo shouted as he swooped out of the building and grabbed Scourge.

Desolate shot her hooks and chains out toward Angelo's feet to save her sister, but Angeline intercepted the chains and swung them and Desolate into a building in the opposite direction.

Before Bane could react, Jeff whistled at her. "Hey, over her 'Little Miss Red,'" he said. "There are two heroes in here you can try to kill."

Bane watched Angelo and Scourge slam through the street and into the sewers. The street caved in at the impact site a moments later.

Bane saw Desolate's chains whipping around in the building across the street and figured her sister would be able to hold her own in a fight against Angeline.

Bane turned back to the building Jeff and Wiseman J were in and smiled. *Surely I can take the two heroes who have no powers,* she thought to herself.

Two shiny sickles, with red handles, appeared in her hands as she flew into the hole and landed on the floor that she had last seen Jeff.

As Bane looked around, she spotted Wiseman J, typing quickly on several computers inside an office in the far corner.

She sneered and floated toward the office.

"Time to die," she whispered.

"Not for him, it isn't," Jeff said as he slammed his staff into the back of Bane's head, sending her tumbling over into a pillar. "For you, however, I'd say it's a big possibility."

Pieces of the 21st floor fell around Angeline as Desolate whipped her chains around in a desperate effort to catch the heroine.

"Stop…moving," Desolate said.

Angeline stared at Desolate and used her telekinesis to send the demoness flying through a large, thick wall.

Desolate seemed unfazed by the attack, whipping her chains around more wildly as she walked out of the debris of the wall and tried to catch Angeline.

Angeline fired three purity arrows, one after the other, toward Desolate. The arrows struck the demoness' right hand and arm, which burnt up in an instant.

Desolate's screams echoed several blocks as she used the chains from her left hand to knock Angeline through several walls and out of the building. Once her chains recoiled into her left hand, Desolate violently ripped off her right arm.

Five small chains, with hooks on the ends, wrapped around a longer, thicker chain, which had rolled out of the wound in Desolate's right shoulder. The smaller chains stiffened around the thicker chain, like muscles made out of metal.

The thicker chain made its way to Desolate's waistline and separated into five smaller chains, which resembled fingers. The smaller chains each went through the links of the larger chains until Desolate's new metal right hand was complete.

"This is so much better," Desolate said as Angeline flew back into the building. "Flesh is so limiting."

"Well, let's get rid of the rest of it," Angeline said as she pulled out her sais.

"I was hoping you would go first," Desolate said as she opened her new chained hand. Each finger shot out razor sharp chains that flew toward Angeline.

Angeline swatted two of the chains away, but two of the chains ripped through her left shoulder and the last one cut her across her right thigh.

"OWWWWW!" Angeline yelled as she dropped her sais and pulled the chains out of her shoulder.

"That's right, little girl," Desolate said. "Feel that pain. Let those lovely screams out."

Large drops of sweat hit the office floor as Jeff tried to keep up with Bane and avoid getting impaled by her sickles.

But she was quick and every now and then, Jeff got sliced by one.

"You can't keep this up for much longer, mortal," Bane said before licking Jeff's blood off one of her sickles. "Mmmmm…that's some tasty blood you have there. I can't wait to taste your organs."

Bane moved at super speed and Jeff tried to follow her with his eyes as she flittered around the room.

"What's the matter?" Bane asked as her voice across the room. "Can't keep up? Getting dizzy? Becoming frightened? All of the above?

Yep, all of the above, Jeff thought. *But, I've got to buy J more time to find out where the Demon Master is.*

"I can do this for as long as you can," Jeff said. "So, how about you stop running around and face me like a real demoness or are you just your sister Scourge's lackey?"

Bane ran into Jeff and threw him through a desk.

"I am no one's lackey," Bane said as she stood over Jeff. "They, however…"

A group of eight elite demon soldiers stormed in from the stairwell and saluted Bane. Bane waved her hand at them as they lowered theirs' and a pair of sickles appeared in their hands.

The demon soldiers turned toward the office Wiseman J was working in and marched toward him.

"While I eat you," Bane said, "they'll cut your mentor into tiny pieces so I'll have some dessert after the main course."

"Guys, I could really use some help over here," Jeff said into his earpiece.

"Very quickly," Wiseman J said as he moved desks and other office furniture in front of the office door.

"I'm...really...busy," Angeline said back.

"On my way," Angelo said.

The building shook violently as Angelo blasted through the floor, causing Bane to stumble back and fall.

"Here," Angelo said as he helped Jeff up and handed Jeff his shield. "Use it and finish her quickly. I'll take care of the demon soldiers."

The demon soldiers turned around and attempted to fight back as Angelo destroyed them one by one.

"Okay, Bane," Jeff said as he twirled his staff in his right hand and carried Angelo's shield in his left hand. "Let's get this over with. I have places to go, ladies to meet."

Bane floated off the ground, gripping her sickles, and raced toward Jeff.

Jeff spun around and slammed the shield into Bane's face.

She screamed as the shield burned her face and ashes formed.

"NOOOOO," Bane screamed. "I will not be defeated like this!"

Bane made a stack of sickles appear beside her and hurled them at super speed toward Jeff.

Jeff twirled his staff, faster than he had ever twirled it before. *There's no way I'm going to be able to catch each one of them.*

But, as each sickle got inches from reaching Jeff, they dropped to the floor with a loud clang. What Bane and Jeff could not see was Angelo, at super speed, catching each of the sickles that Jeff's staff could not.

When Bane stopped throwing the sickles, Jeff stopped twirling his staff and smiled.

"Impossible," Bane said as beads of sweat and blood dripped from her face.

"Not when your pal can move at super speed," Jeff said as Angelo helped Wiseman J out of the office. "While he was moving at super speed, he was able to make this for me…"

In Jeff's left hand, where he had been holding Angelo's shield, was a shimmering sickle, made out of purity bombs.

Bane couldn't make the weapon out, only seeing bright lights as Jeff threw the weapon toward her chest. By the time Bane tried to move, it was too late.

She didn't scream as her body was engulfed into flames and burned into ashes.

Jeff fell on his knees and let out a deep sigh as he turned toward Angelo and Wiseman J. "I am so glad that is over."

The three men didn't see the red vapor seep from the burning ashes, through the hole, run down the side of the building and through a sewer grate.

"Good job, Jeff," Angelo said as he looked out the hole in the building. He could see Desolate's chains violently tearing through the walls and floors of the building across the street. "I need to go help Angeline. You two stay safe."

"We will," Jeff said as he watched Angelo smash through the building Desolate and Angeline were fighting in.

"Come, Jeff," Wiseman J said as he headed back into the office. "I think I'm close to pinpointing the Demon Master's location."

"Thank God," Angeline said as Angelo burst through the wall and slammed his shield into Desolate's back.

The demoness tumbled but regained her footing in an instant and furiously whipped her chains around again.

"What happened to her arm?" Angelo asked as he dodged the falling debris from the floors above.

"She upgraded it," Angeline said.

"Are you all right?" Angelo asked as he noticed the blood stains around the shoulder area of Angeline's clothing.

"Yeah, it healed a few minutes ago," Angeline said. "Take my advice: don't let those chains go through you."

"I'LL KILL YOU ALL!" Desolate screamed as her chains tore through more of the building.

"She's desperate," Angeline said as she avoided more falling debris. "She's gonna bring this entire building down."

"Let's help her," Angelo said.

Angelo pulled his sword out and pulled it apart into two separate swords.

"We're going to pin her with our weapons, like I did her sister and brother," Angelo said.

Angeline gave Angelo a concerned look. "You're not going to get all dark and scary and start glowing red on a mass-destruction level again, are you?"

"No," Angelo said, handing her his swords. "Just use your telekinesis and use my swords and your sais to keep her in the center of this floor, or what's left of it."

"What are you going to do?"

"I'll be back in a few seconds to tell you," Angelo said as he flew out of the building.

"Looks like someone's boyfriend ditched her," Desolate said.

"It would appear that way," Angeline said as she tossed Angelo's swords on the ground. She threw her sais on the ground next to them. "But, you're wrong."

"Make sure you pin her chains to the support beams," Angelo said through Angeline's earpiece.

Desolate made the chains of her new hand shoot out toward Angeline.

Angeline held her right hand out, causing Angelo's swords and her sais to shake violently as she used her telekinesis to control them.

As Desolate's chains got closer and closer, the weapons flew into the air and each slipped through several links of an incoming chain.

Angelo's swords flew into the ceiling in the middle of the office space as Angeline's sais flew into the floor.

Desolate screamed as she attempted to pull the chains back, especially after Angeline caught the fifth chain with her right hand.

"If you want them back, you'll have to kill me," Angeline said.

Desolate grinned as three small amber, hooked chains slowly slid out of the palm of her left hand and she leapt at Angeline.

"I'm ready," Angelo said on the other end of Angeline's earpiece. "As soon as you're ready, blast the center of the ceiling with your telekinesis and stand back."

"Okay," Angeline said.

"Okay, what?" Desolate asked as she got closer and closer to where Angeline and her right hand chains were.

The chains of Desolate's left hand circled the office space and came in fast behind Angeline as Desolate got closer to Angeline.

"This," Angeline said as she lifted her hands toward the ceiling.

As Angeline did, the three chains of Desolate's left hand reached her, with two hooking into Angeline's arms and a third one into her neck.

Desolate, with a giant murderous grin on her face, was now in Angeline's face.

"I could kill you now," Desolate said. "But, I want you to suffer slow and painfully, just like you were going to make me do."

Angeline looked at the ceiling above her and Desolate and concentrated.

"That...won't...be...happening...today," Angeline said as her telekinesis caused the ceiling to collapse onto her and Desolate. Hundreds of shiny little balls of light, which followed the debris, showered onto them as well.

Desolate ripped her chains out of Angeline and tried to shield herself, but it didn't work. The small purity bombs Angelo had piled up above the ceiling were burrowing their way into Desolate's body.

"Noooooooo," Desolate moaned. She fell to the ground and convulsed as her body glowed white and her chains followed suit.

Angelo flew out of the hole in the ceiling and landed next to Angeline as Desolate's chains ripped their weapons out of the walls, freeing her.

The heroes willed their weapons to return to them and flew out of the building as Desolate's chains whipped around, which brought the entire building down on her.

Angelo and Angeline landed on the street below and watched as Desolate's burning body turned into ashes and the building's debris spilled over into the street.

"Smart idea," Angeline said, patting Angelo on the back.

"Couldn't have done it without you," Angelo said.

Neither of the heroes noticed the amber vapor leaving the debris and heading into a manhole cover.

A few seconds later, the ground shook violently and a female scream echoed from beneath Angelo and Angeline.

"Let me guess," Angeline said. "You didn't kill Scourge, did you?"

"After I flew her down into the ground, we got separated," Angelo said. "I tried to find her for a few minutes, but then Jeff called for backup..."

"Which means she's ready for revenge," Angeline said.

The ground shook again as 25 elite demon soldiers clawed their way out from under the street in front of Angelo and Angeline and attacked the heroes.

Another loud female scream shot into the air, this time filled with agony and sorrow. It echoed from the intersection down the street from where Angelo and Angeline were fighting the elite demon soldiers.

Jeff watched the fight through his binoculars. He panned down the street behind Angelo and Angeline and saw Scourge, disheveled and with red, amber and dark blue energy crackling around her body. As she flew out of the street, Scourge looked at Angelo and Angeline and then, with a sharp snap of her head, up toward Jeff.

"J, we got to get out of here...now," Jeff said as Scourge flew toward him. He ran from the hole and followed Wiseman J to the stairwell door.

Jeff looked over his shoulder, bumping into and nearly tumbling over Wiseman J.

"Why did you stop, J?" Jeff asked as he turned around toward J and the stairwell.

There J was, about four feet off the ground and being choked to death, with one hand by Scourge. Her face was charred on one side and most of her hair was gone. Her clothes were tattered and dark and bloody bruises were scattered across her body.

Jeff made his staff extend and jammed it into Scourge's armpit, forcing her to drop Wiseman J.

"RUN, J!" Jeff screamed as he pushed his mentor away and furiously attacked Scourge.

Scourge said nothing as she moved at super speed, delivering punch after punch into Jeff's unprotected head and chest.

But, Jeff attempted to counter her attacks and deliver a few of his own.

Wiseman J ran to the hole and looked down at Angelo and Angeline as they fought and destroyed the elite demon soldiers.

"We need help up here immediately," Wiseman J said into his earpiece. "I don't know how long Jeff can hold Scourge off."

Wiseman J saw Angelo tilt his head up toward him.

"We'll be there in a few seconds," Angelo said. "We just have a few more to put down."

"Please hurry," J said as he turned around and watched Scourge throw Jeff through tables, filing cabinets and chairs.

"For one without powers, you are very strong, Jeff: Ward of Law," Scourge said. "But, it's not enough."

Jeff did his best to crawl under some tossed over furniture, trying to put some distance between himself and Scourge.

But, Scourge just threw the furniture to another area of the office space and continued after Jeff.

"You three killed my sisters," Scourge said as she pulled out her scourges and whipped Jeff.

He tried to block the whips with his staff, but it didn't work. The whips of the scourges tore through his military fatigues and his flesh.

Wiseman J decided he could no longer stand by and do nothing. "HEY! IT'S ME YOUR MASTER WANTS DEAD!" he shouted.

Scourge whipped her body around toward Wiseman J, threw her scourges down and made a large sickle appear in her right hand.

"You're absolutely right," Scourge said as she threw the sickle toward Wiseman J.

Scourge smiled as the sickle sliced through Wiseman J's chest and tore through his heart, killing him instantly.

She watched as Wiseman J 's lifeless body fell to the ground and right as she was about to laugh aloud, she jerked forward as Jeff's glowing white staff shot through her chest and caused her body to ignite.

Scourge turned to face Jeff, whose face was so swollen, he was unrecognizable. She raised her hand to smash his head into the floor and kill him, but as she did, Angeline's sai flew through the back of her head.

Scourge couldn't scream as the purity burn quickly rushed across her face and turned her head into ashes.

The rest of Scourge's body burned into ashes as Angelo and Angeline landed inside the building.

Angelo raced over to Jeff's side.

"Is he…?" Angeline was afraid to finish her question.

Angelo checked Jeff's pulse. "He's alive. Barely. Sounds like he's struggling to breathe and he's unconscious.

"How's J?" Angelo asked as he gently picked up Jeff and placed him on a nearby couch.

Jeff shook uncontrollably. Angelo found a blanket and placed it over him.

"I think he's going into shock," Angelo said.

"Angeline?"

Angelo knew something was wrong before he turned around. Angeline had not said anything and then he heard her cry.

Angelo walked over to her and found her cradling Wiseman J's head in her lap. The sickle that had killed J remained inside his chest.

"He's…gone," Angeline said as tears fell from her face unto Wiseman J's. "He's gone."

Angelo fell to his knees, placed his left hand in Wiseman J's right hand and wept.

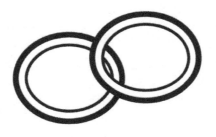

End:

Light Against Darkness

Tyrone Tony Reed Jr.

13

Interlude: An Angelic Assist

Five minutes before Kevin and Juanita

returned home from Dark Earth...

A bright, white portal opened high above Riverside Drive, just below the cloudy skies. A being made of white light floated out of the portal and the portal quickly closed behind him. The glowing being looked around the city and its light glowed brighter and brighter, but it was invisible to the natural eye.

Home, the being thought. *My real home and my real time...and I know nothing about it, because I was ripped away from my parents...my sister...my twin brother...and replaced by an abomination that lived only a couple of hours, because the Demon Master wanted revenge on my brother. Because of him...I...who I would have been...who I was supposed to be...no longer exist in this world.*

The light around the being briefly turned orange and then returned to white as the being concentrated and calmed down.

But, one day...and hopefully, very soon...I will be reunited with my family and future-in-law...

The being's thoughts were interrupted by a large beam of blue light shooting out of the clouds and into the Art Pola branch of the Memphis Public Library.

S.O.L.A.D.™: It's Just the Beginning

"They're back," the being said as he watched two white streaks of light, side by side, travel down the beam of blue light and into the library. "It's time."

A few seconds later, the being watched as a red streak of light traveled down the beam of light and shot out of it just before it reached the library's roof. The light flew over the city before landing on the roof of a tall building. The red light grew for a few seconds before exploding. Once the light faded, six, large, human-like figures stood where the red light had landed.

One figure, with glowing orange eyes, stepped forward and raised its hands toward the sky. The already cloudy sky became filled with darker, ominous clouds as hundreds of streaks of lightning and booms of thunder shook the entire city very hard. The large buildings in downtown Memphis swayed and the

Mississippi River crashed onto the bank of Tom Lee Park, flooding Riverside Dr. and Mud Island.

"And now, he's here," the being of white light said. "Right on schedule."

Eight large and violently fast tornadoes rotated out of the clouds and touched down into the Mississippi River. Four of the tornadoes headed south on the Mississippi River toward the Memphis-Arkansas Bridge, while the other four tornadoes headed north toward the Hernando de Soto Bridge. Once the tornadoes reached their respective bridges, the tornadoes lined up along the bridges and once the figure with orange eyes clapped his hands together, the tornadoes destroyed the bridges, killing hundreds of people.

The being of light turned away in sorrow and lowered his head. *Lord, I know what part I am to play in this day. Please give me the strength to only intervene where you have told me to and to not get full of myself and decide to take action where you have not called me to. Amen.*

The figure with orange eyes then looked to the skies as he stretched his hands toward it. A red mist flew from his hands and into the clouds, briefly giving them a red tint before they returned to their natural color.

You only get to attack this city, Monster, not the world, the being of light thought as he waved his hands toward the city of Memphis.

An invisible sphere grew over the clouds and the entire city, stopping the red mist from spreading higher into the air and out of the city. Once the sphere was complete, the red mist attached to it, trying to break out, but it was unable to.

Flames shot out of the corners of the orange eyes of the evil figure as he pumped his hands in the air, willing his red mist to break through the sphere. But, with every pump of his hands, it became more apparent that his attempts were in vain.

The figure with orange eyes growled, waved his hands around to his sides and the red mist expanded and responded. The excess of the red mist flew along the sides of the sphere and split from the main part of the mist. A few seconds later, hundreds of individual pockets of excess mist began twirling and forming tornadoes along the sphere.

No one gets out alive, the figure with orange eyes said to the other figures telepathically. *Have fun with the heroes, but remember…they are mine to destroy.*

As the words resounded in their minds, the figures each pointed to several tornadoes, creating red portals within them. Thousands of demon soldiers, regular demons and demon dogs leapt out of the tornadoes and began attacking, killing and eating the people throughout the city.

S.O.L.A.D.™: It's Just the Beginning

Let us begin... the figure with orange eyes said as the other figures formed a circle around him. The wind blew and became stronger and stronger as all six figures began to merge together and formed a large black tornado. The tornado floated off the rooftop and merged with the dark clouds in the sky. A few moments later, the tornado had disappeared into the clouds.

The being of light focused his super eyesight and spotted Kevin and Juanita running out of the Art Pola Library. The being looked back over his shoulder as an enormous black dragon emerged out of the clouds and circled downtown Memphis.

A man ran frantically up to Kevin and Juanita and, with his super hearing, the being heard the man say "The end is here! The end is here!" As the man ran away, the being saw Kevin and Juanita run into an alley next to the library and saw flashes of blue and yellow light come from within the alley a few seconds later.

The being slowly flew backwards into a white portal that opened up behind him.

The war has begun... the being said as the portal began to close. He could see Angelo and Angeline, with their weapons drawn, flying toward the dragon. *Let's get to work.*

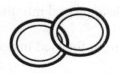

Four seconds after Angelo

was impaled by three spears...

A portal of white light opened over the street in front of the Art Pola Library and the being of white light floated out of it, unseen.

He watched as Angelo fell to his knees and his crimson blood spilled from around the spears in his stomach. The being of light heard the Demon Master telepathically tell Angelo to die as hellholes began to burst open at the ends of the street.

Stand up, brother, the being of light said as he held his hands down toward Angelo. White light surrounded Angelo and Angelo began to stand. The white light caused the spears to shake and slowly slide back to the front of Angelo's belly.

Now, brother, the being of light said telepathically. *Tell Angeline to drop her force field now.*

The being of light heard Angelo's shout and telekinetically pulled the now glowing white, wooden spears out of Angelo's stomach at super speed. He directed the spears to fly around Angelo, Angeline and Jeff as the demon soldiers marched toward them.

Soon, the demon soldiers could not stop their advance as the spears created a glowing white vortex, which pulled the demon soldiers into it.

That's it, the being of light thought as he watched the Demon Master move behind his lieutenants for protection.

Two of the spears broke off from the vortex and hovered over the hellholes. They twirled over them, snuffing out the flames and closing the portals inside.

The being of light clapped his hands hard. The impact of the clap sounded like thunder and caused the spears over the hellholes to explode. The pieces rained down over the hellholes, creating barriers that finished closing them.

Once the bright white light of the explosion faded away, the being of light commanded the last spear to float over the Demon Master and his lieutenants.

I could end this all now, the being of light thought as he watched them shake. He dwelled on the idea of impaling each and every one of the lieutenants before impaling the Demon Master and causing the spear to explode inside of him.

But…this is not my battle and I am not the one who is supposed to defeat you, the being of light thought. *Even so…I can still have a little fun…*

The being of light clapped his hands together and the spear exploded, taking out the remaining demon soldiers. The Demon Master and his lieutenants were safe from the shrapnel as it hit a red force field they stood under.

Your end will come soon enough, the being of light said as he floated backwards into a white portal. *Very soon.*

Three minutes before Jeff faced off against Belicista…

An unseen, white portal opened onto the tarmac of the Memphis International Airport in front of a large airliner filled with frightened passengers. The unseen being of white light floated out of it and around the airliner as the portal closed.

As he came around the other side, he spotted a young, black woman, with brown hair and familiar eyes, looking out the window at the demons, demon dogs and demon soldiers attacking the airport.

*It's her…my sister…*the being of light thought. *I only know her from the fractured memories I was shown…but it is her…*

The being of light's super hearing interrupted his thoughts as he picked up the frantic conversation that the pilot and co-pilot were having with the Air Traffic Control Tower.

"Why can't we just come up to the gate or exit the plane from here?" the pilot, Captain Dana Fox, asked into her headset.

"Captain Fox, the airport is under attack," said a voice on the other end of the headset. "People are getting killed by monsters."

The co-pilot, Captain Scully Mulder shook his head and tried not to curse at the air traffic controller.

"Look, we have been stuck on the tarmac for two hours and we've got passengers on the plane who said their friends and families have already called them about groups of monsters attacking the city," Mulder said. "Sitting out here in the open isn't exactly safe. Our passengers are scared and frankly, after what we've seen on the news apps on our phones, we are too."

Static grew in the headsets of the pilots, but they could hear screams in the control tower.

"Hello?" Fox asked. "What's going on up there?"

The pilots looked up at the tower through the airplane's windshield and could see flying demon soldiers pulling people out of the tower and eating them. More flying demons could be seen in the distance, heading northeast from downtown Memphis and flying toward the airport.

The pilots and passengers of the other airplanes on the tarmac opened the main doors and the emergency exits and started sliding down the evacuation chutes. As they did, flying demon soldiers swooped down upon them and the demon dogs leapt onto them from behind.

"I don't care what control tower said, we need to get these people out of here and to safety," Fox said as she maneuvered the airplane toward the airport. "We can access that terminal in front of us."

The being of light watched as a group of flying demon soldiers landed on Patricia's airplane and began tearing it open.

S.O.L.A.D.™: It's Just the Beginning

Lord, I cannot stand back and watch as these beasts kill my sister and the other passengers, the being of light prayed. *I know you sent me specifically here to help my brother and his future wife, but don't let it be at the cost of my sister's life...Not like it was in the past of my new home. Please allow me to save these people, especially her. Why else would you have opened the portal here during this war?*

The being of light's body flashed twice and a white, shining sword appeared in each of his hands.

The being of light lifted his head toward the dark cloudy sky and thought, *Thank you, Lord. I will not fail you.*

He rushed to Patricia's plane and destroyed the demon soldiers in the blink of an eye.

While the pilots lined up with the terminal doors, the being of light landed on the ground and took out the demon soldiers that were running and flying toward the plane.

None of you are going to make it to any more planes or that airport, the being of light thought as he joined the hilts of his swords together to form a lance. The lance shot out of his hands in a flash and soared into the dark, stormy clouds above the airport.

All of the demon soldiers ceased their attacks and gazed up at the twirling clouds that had turned bright white. The ones flying in the skies began to get pulled into the swirling vortex. They desperately tried to stay away from the vortex, some sacrificing a fellow flying demon soldier in an attempt to gain enough momentum to make it to the ground. But, it was pointless.

Seconds later, the demon soldiers, regular demons and demon dogs on the ground were also caught up.

A giant demon soldier slammed one of his battle-axes into the ground and then slammed the other into the ground. In quick succession, the demon soldier made his way to the tail of Patricia's plane. He once again slammed the battle-axe into the ground and used his other battle-axe to slash a giant hole in the back of the airplane.

The giant demon solider climbed into the cabin of the plane and began dismembering people. The sight of bloody flesh hanging from skeletons caused the passengers to climb over one another, trying to avoid becoming the demon soldier's next victim.

One of the passengers climbed over was a five-year-old, black boy, who had gotten separated from his mother in the panic and chaos. The little boy had backed into a row of seats near the middle of the plane and sat there in a fetal position, shaking as tears ran down his terrified face.

"MOM!" the little boy screamed as passengers ran past him and climbed over each other and the seats to get out of the plane.

"MOMMY!" the boy shouted again, his screams being drowned out by the screams of the victims of the giant demon soldier, who was making his bloody trek toward the front of the plane.

Once the giant demon soldier made his way to the middle section of the plane, the little boy screamed at the sight of the behemoth, which had blood dripping from his mouth and bloody battle-axes in each hand.

"MOMMY, HELP!" the little boy screamed as he threw his hands up to his face and covered his eyes.

The giant demon soldier laughed and the gruffness of his voice echoed throughout the plane like 10 loud bass speakers pushed beyond their limits.

"Mommy can't help you now, boy," the giant demon soldier said as he dropped the battle-axe, in his right hand, onto the seats behind him. "You're mine."

A suitcase was slammed into the giant demon soldier's face, followed by a fire extinguisher, as he reached for the little boy with his giant, bloody hands.

"Leave him alone, monster," Patricia said as she stood a few feet away and held a suitcase over her head. "Or I'll beat you to death with this luggage."

The giant demon soldier leaned back and laughed.

"Well, come on then, little lady," the giant demon soldier said. "After I eat you, I'll use his bones to pick your remains out of my teeth."

"I don't think so," the being of light said from behind the giant demon soldier as he cut off the behemoth's right arm with a glowing white sword.

The giant demon soldier screamed and swung around with the battle-axe in his left hand, trying to strike the being of light.

But the being of light ducked, allowing the battle-axe to fly over him. He stood up after it had passed and severed the left arm of the giant demon soldier.

The being of light jabbed his sword into the behemoth's chest before the giant demon soldier could react again and the giant demon soldier instantly burst into ashes.

The being of light walked through the ashes and extended his right hand to the little boy.

"He's gone now," the being of light said as the glow of his body faded away. He appeared to be a man in his 30s, wearing a white shirt and white jeans. "You're safe now."

The little boy jumped into his arms and the being of light, who now looked like a regular person, handed the boy to Patricia.

"I'm sure she'll help you find your mom," he said as he looked up at Patricia.

Patricia gasped as she looked into the face of the man.

"What is it?" the man asked.

"I don't know," Patricia said. "You look and sound a lot like my baby brother Kevin, but, you look a few years older than me."

The man smiled and walked toward the hole in the back of the plane. "I get that a lot back home."

"Wait," Patricia said as she held the little boy in her arms. "Who are you?"

"Just someone doing what he was called to do," the man said as a portal opened up behind him. His body began to glow again with a blinding, white light. "Be safe."

The man floated into the portal and seconds later, the portal closed.

Patricia thought for a second about what the man had said. *What did he mean by, "I get that a lot?"*

The remaining passengers got off the plane and Patricia and the little boy, now walking by her side and holding on to her left hand, followed.

Patricia knelt in front of the little boy and smiled once they reached the terminal.

"Sweetheart, everything is going to be okay," she said as she wiped away a tear from his eye. "I just need you to tell me your name so we can find your mom."

The little boy wiped his face with his hands, shivered for a second and said, "My name is Jerry…Jerry Wiseman."

Two seconds after Angelo was

surrounded by Scourge and her sisters...

I don't want to die like this, were the thoughts that the being of light heard in his mind as he flew out of a white portal, which opened on the backside of 100 North Main. They were Angelo's thoughts, which echoed with feelings of agony, fear and regret throughout the mind of the being of light.

Without hesitation, the being of light quickly created a large, bright, white ball of light in his right hand and threw it toward the building.

It's okay, my brother, the being of light said. *Let me save you like you did for me, so many years ago. I owe you that and so much more...especially since you found me…beyond your time…when others thought I was long dead.*

The ball of light quickly encased Angelo and burned brightly, searing the flesh of Scourge, Bane and Desolate as the demonesses screamed and sought cover. The ball of light zipped out of the building and flew down to the SUV waiting in front of the building.

The being of light flew around the building, once again unseen, and saw Angeline emerge from the sunroof of the SUV.

Not this time, sister-in-law, the being of light said as he pointed his right index finger toward her, creating an invisible barrier around her that blocked her telekinesis. *You soon will learn to hate that I can do that.*

With his left hand, the being of light guided the ball of light, which encased Angelo, into the SUV. A second later, the being of light made an explosion gesture with his right hand and the light shot out of the SUV and disintegrated the demon soldiers in the immediate area.

Only two more stops now and then back home, the being of light said as Scourge, Desolate and Bane flew out of the debris, passed him and chased after the SUV. *I wish I could have done more…I wish I could have prevented what happens next, especially for my wife…*

One hour after Wiseman J was killed by Scourge…

The office where Wiseman J's body lied was dark and every once and a while, pieces of debris fell down from the ceiling. A trail of blood led from the office out into the rest of the floor of the building.

A white portal opened up and the being of light walked out and stepped into the office.

She's going to be sad that you're gone, the being of light said as he knelt beside the body. *She only got a year with you…a year she loved and cherished after I found her and brought her back to you.*

He gently lifted the body into his arms and stood up. The portal reopened and the being of light used his telekinesis to float the body into the portal. *We will give you a homegoing of a hero, which you are.*

The portal whirled around faster, waiting for the being of light to enter it. But, the being of light flew past the portal and out of the building.

Not yet, he said. *I want to look at the city one more time before my final assignment.*

The being of light flew just above the clouds and spotted Angeline and Angelo hovering over the FedEx Forum.

The end draws near, the being of light thought. *It's up to you two now. Time for me to go back to my new home… after I pick up Jeff.*

A new portal opened before the being of light and he floated into it. A second later, it closed.

14

Far From Safe

"**W**e have to go," Angelo said as he wiped the tears from his eyes and stood up. "It's time to finish this.'"

Angeline lowered Wiseman J's head to the floor and joined Angelo as he looked out of the hole in the building's wall. She looked back at Jeff, whose breaths had gotten shorter and shorter.

"We have to get Jeff some help first," Angeline said as she walked over to the couch Jeff lied on.

"I can see ambulance lights bouncing off the buildings down the street," Angelo said. "There's probably a triage set up down there. We can take Jeff there."

"What about J?"Angeline asked as she looked over at his body.

Angelo's head dropped and a tear fell from his cheek to the floor.

"I'll put his…body in the office in the corner," Angelo said. "It…he…will be safe there until this is over."

"I'm not sure I can keep this up," Angeline said as she watched Angelo pick up Wiseman J's body.

Wiseman J's right hand fell and Angeline let out a small sob as Angelo passed her and headed to the office.

"We have to," Angelo said. "Our city is counting on us. Jeff is counting on us."

Angelo laid Wiseman J's body down on a comforter in the corner office and covered his body up with the remainder of the comforter.

He walked out and closed the door behind him.

"J... he believed in us," Angelo said as walked over to the couch and picked up Jeff. "We can't let him down."

"We already did," Angeline said as she wiped tears from her eyes.

Angelo didn't look at her as he carried Jeff to the hole.

"He would say that the only way we could ever let him down is if we fail to save our city," Angelo said.

Angeline walked over to Angelo and stood beside him.

"That's what he would have said," Angeline said. "But, I'm serious... I'm very tired and I don't feel as strong as I did a couple of hours ago."

"Neither do I," Angelo said. "But, you and I know that the law enforcement can't beat the Demon Master and his army. We are the only ones who have a chance to get him out of our city and off of our world."

Angeline nodded.

"Let's go," she said.

A few minutes later, Angelo, with Jeff still in his arms, landed at the intersection of Monroe Avenue and South Main Street.

Angelo walked over to the lobby of One Commerce Square and stood close to the building. Angeline followed him.

"What is it?" Angeline asked.

The heroes heard screams, growls and gunfire as they stood next to the building.

"We need to stay low and find a place to put Jeff before we fight any more demon soldiers," Angelo said.

"They're definitely nearby," Angeline said.

"Put a force field around Jeff and place him in this lobby," Angelo said.

Jeff floated out of Angelo's arms as Angeline used her telekinesis and a purple force field formed around him. The force field floated away from the two heroes and went deep inside the lobby.

Angeline focused her gaze on some furniture in the lobby and telekinetically lifted them and placed them gently on top of her force field. She focused on some more furniture and telekinetically moved them up against the front doors and windows of the lobby.

"There," Angeline said. "He should be safe in there."

Angelo motioned for her to follow him as he stuck close to the buildings and walked down South Main Street, crossing General Washburn's Escape Alley and then turning left at the intersection of South Main Street and Union Avenue.

The heroes walked east on the empty streets of Union Avenue, finding three abandoned ambulances in the middle of the street. They could still hear screams and gunfire, which were coming from the east.

"No triage here," Angeline said.

"No," Angelo said as he pulled his sword out. "It's a trap."

A group of demon soldiers, perched on the rooftops of the buildings that lined the street, before the intersection of Highway 14 and Union Avenue, leapt down to the street, growled and drooled as they looked upon the heroes.

"These ambulance decoys have sent us more tasty morsels, my comrades," a large, gray demon soldier said. His stomach poked out, giving off the impression that he had eaten a few minutes before the heroes' arrival.

Angeline pulled out her sais and threw one into his stomach. The sai went through the demon soldier's armor and into the demon soldier, which burned into ashes in an instant. Inside the ashes sat a pile of undigested human bones.

"Are those...?" Angeline struggled to get her words out.

"It's the remains of the people they lured here," Angelo said.

"And you two are about to join them," said another large demon soldier as he walked up to Angeline. "I'll eat you first and let the others fight over your friend."

"Eat this," Angeline said as she shoved her sai upward into the demon soldier's chin.

The demon soldier's head burst into bright white and orange flames and the rest of his body ignited seconds later.

The remaining demon soldiers attacked Angelo and Angeline, but they destroyed the demons with ease, leaving several piles of ashes and human bones behind.

Angeline walked over to the ambulances, reached into the cabin and turned off the emergency and strobe lights.

Angelo looked inside the back of one of the ambulances and slammed the doors shut as Angeline came to the back.

"What is it?"

"You don't want to look in there," he said.

"More remains?" Angeline asked.

Angelo nodded.

Angeline waved her hands toward the ambulances and the ambulances slid out of the street and to the side of a nearby building.

Angeline balled her hands up and the lights on the ambulances shattered, as if being crushed by an invisible force.

"They don't get to do that trick again," she said as she and Angelo continued walking east on Union Ave.

The sounds of gunfire, demonic growls and people screaming grew louder.

Angeline pointed up toward The Peabody Hotel and Angelo followed her finger up to the rooftop, where several National Guardsmen were shooting at flying demon soldiers that were circling the hotel.

The heroes stayed close to the buildings as they walked onto Third Street and came near the front of the hotel.

Once there, they saw concrete barricades surrounding the hotel and armed soldiers and police officers shooting at demon soldiers, which were attacking from the air and from the ground.

The flying demon soldiers crashed through the windows of the hotel, and a few seconds later, emerged with one or two half-eaten people in their talons. The demon soldiers smiled as blood dripped from their lips and onto the streets below.

Neither Angelo nor Angeline said a word to each other as they flew up alongside the hotel, fighting the demon soldiers and trying to protect the remaining people inside and outside the hotel.

"The angels are here," shouted one soldier on the rooftop as he watched Angeline slam two demon soldiers into the building and stabbed them with her sais. The demon soldiers burst into flames and ashes and the soldiers on the rooftop burst into cheers.

"All right, men," an army sergeant said. "Cover the angels and try to at least wound some of these monsters."

Angeline smiled at the sergeant and the soldiers and flew around to the other side of the hotel.

"Sounds like we have some air and ground support," Angeline said.

"Every bit helps," Angelo said as he cut through six demon soldiers in front of the barricades. "But, we need to wrap this up quickly. We still need to get Jeff to a hospital."

"I've got an idea," Angeline said. "What if I do the force field bubble thing I did earlier, but this time, on a much larger scale and reverse it to spread out a few blocks?"

"You think you got enough energy for that?"

"I think so," Angeline said. "I'll clear the floors of any remaining demon soldiers while you get your purity bombs ready."

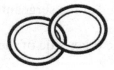

After destroying a few more demon soldiers, Angelo flew high above the Peabody Hotel and Angeline landed in front of it.

"I'm going inside now," Angeline said into her earpiece. "Get ready."

Angeline walked into the hotel's lobby and saw the Peabody Ducks, huddled under a bar with a bartender.

"It's okay," she said to them. "We're about to make sure everything is right again."

Three flying demon soldiers crashed through the lobby doors and the soldiers outside shot at them.

Angeline flew toward the demons and attacked them.

"I GOT IT," Angeline shouted to the soldiers as bullets bounced off various parts of her body.

The soldiers ceased firing and Angeline fired three arrows into the three demon soldiers.

"You're one of the angels they've been talking about on the news, aren't you?" the bartender asked.

"Yes," Angeline said. "Just stay right there for now until I can guarantee that it's safe to come out."

Angeline held her hands up and then lowered them to her sides. As she did, a purple force field appeared over the hotel's rooftop and formed around the hotel.

When the force field connected with the street, Angelo, who flew outside the force field, dropped purity bombs on the force field. The purity bombs rolled down the force field, stacked neatly on top of each other and connected.

A group of demon soldiers swooped down on Angelo, who pulled out his sword and sliced through them.

"There are more demon soldiers on the way," Angelo said. "The bottom half of the force field is filled with purity bombs and I'm working on the top half."

"Well, I can't keep this up too much longer," Angeline said as she watched the Peabody Ducks waddled over to her, looked at her face, walked over to the marble fountain and jumped in.

The Peabody Ducks swam around in the fountain's water and quacked loudly.

"They must feel pretty safe with you around," the bartender said as he brought Angeline a glass of water.

"Thanks," Angeline said as she opened her mouth for the bartender to pour some water into her mouth.

He did and after a few gulps, Angeline had drank it up.

"Want some more?" the bartender asked as he took out a napkin and wiped Angeline's mouth.

"No, thank you," she said. "But those soldiers out there could probably use some."

The bartender motioned for the people hiding in the kitchen and restaurant area to come out.

"I need some help getting some liquid refreshment out to those soldiers," the bartender said.

Liquid refreshment? Angeline thought to herself as she chuckled. *He sounds like Kevin. Thinking of whom…*

"How's it going up there?" Angeline asked into her earpiece.

"Are you talking to me?" the bartender asked.

"No, my partner," Angeline said as she telekinetically moved her hair to show the bartender the earpiece. "He's flying above the hotel."

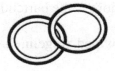

"I'm done," Angelo said as he dropped several purity bombs down on the top of the force field. "Ready when you are."

As the purity bombs snapped into place, the force field glowed and the purple light the force field emitted shined through the purity bombs, making a disco ball effect inside the hotel and across the city.

"Okay," Angeline said. "Here I go."

The force field grew brighter and brighter, causing the purity bombs to glow brighter and brighter. Streams of pure light struck demons all over the city, instantly incinerating them.

"Angeline, don't make your force field spread out," Angelo said. "What you are doing is working out so much better. Just keep that force field's glow going strong."

"I'm trying," Angeline said "but, I'm so tired."

"I know, Angeline," Angelo said. "But, it's worth it. You are making a big difference. Just keep it going a little longer."

Angelo watched as the force field grew brighter and brighter and the light that passed through the purity bombs now shined like spotlight lights as the purity bombs circled the force field.

"Angelo... I need...to stop," Angeline said.

Angelo could tell from the tone in Angeline's voice that something was wrong and that she was losing control.

"Go ahead and stop," Angelo said.

"I...can't," Angeline said. "I can't... sever my... connection... with the force field... and the purity bombs."

"I'm coming," Angelo said as he flew up toward the dome over the city. He hovered just inches away from it and spun around. Once he reached 300 miles per hour, Angelo swooped down toward the hotel and shattered the area of the force field that was several feet away from the lobby entrance.

As Angelo slowed down, some of the soldiers were blown into the lobby by the drafts his super speed had generated.

"Sorry," Angelo said as he ran over to Angeline and the soldiers slid on their backs across the floor.

"I'm here," Angelo said as he looked into Angeline's eyes, which glowed purple.

Angeline's hair blew over her head as she floated a few feet off the ground.

"Angeline, I'm here," Angelo said. "How can I help you?"

"I…don't…know," Angeline said as tears streamed down her face. "I…can't…make it…stop."

"Not alone, you can't," Angelo said as he floated off the ground and slid his hands over hers. "Let me help you."

Angelo closed his eyes, concentrated hard and prayed. *God, I don't know what's happening to Angeline...to Juanita... and I don't know what to do. Please, please, please guide me and show me how to help her and this city. Give me the strength I need to do what needs to be done to protect her and the city.*

Angelo's body glowed white and the white glow spread from his body and across Angeline's body. A few seconds later, Angeline's eyes turned white and her hair fell back down.

"Let me help you do this," Angelo said to Angeline, not really knowing how he could.

In his thoughts, he saw Angeline, overwhelmed by her powers and almost being consumed. But, he called out to her and walked into the winds, which represented her powers, and wrapped his arms around her.

It's okay, Angelo thought. *I'm here with you. Let me help you do this.*

Angelo imagined himself giving Angeline some of his powers, some of his strength and all of his love for her. He imagined them working as one to save the city and not being overcome by the war the Demon Master was waging against them and the city.

Angelo also imagined that he was in control of the force field and the purity bombs. He imagined that each purity bomb had flown off of the force field and sought out a demon to destroy. As he concentrated on that thought, it happened.

Angelo turned his thoughts to the force field, imagining that the force field shined so brightly that its light engulfed the city, taking out every demon that was touched by the light, and it happened.

S.O.L.A.D.™: It's Just the Beginning

A few seconds later, Angelo and Angeline both floated to the floor. Angeline's eyes returned to normal and she hugged Angelo tightly. A passionate kiss on Angelo's lips followed.

Angelo hugged her back and gave Angeline a passionate kiss of his own.

"I felt so lost," Angeline said as Angelo wiped away her tears. "But, I saw you in my thoughts, helping me. And what you thought about with the force field and the purity bombs…Did that actually happen?"

They walked out of the hotel's lobby and saw ashes falling from the sky. The soldiers and people outside cheered.

"Looks like it did," Angelo said before smiling at Angeline.

Angelo's smile disappeared when his super hearing picked up Jeff's shallow breathing through the cheers and applause.

"What is it?" Angeline asked.

"Jeff's breaths are getting slower and shallower. We need to get him to a hospital now."

Angelo flew at super speed, retrieved Jeff and returned a few seconds later.

"There's a triage center at the FedEx Forum," an Army sergeant said when he saw Jeff. "Most of the hospitals were attacked by those monsters and a lot of folks were taken there. I'm sure your friend can get help there. I'll radio ahead and let them know you're coming."

"Thank you, Sergeant…," Angelo said.

"Tyrone David Cheshier-Reed," the sergeant said. "But, it's me that should be thanking you for helping us and saving our lives. Thank God for you two."

"We're all just doing our part to save the city," Angelo said as he and Angeline flew into the air. "Keep up the great work."

Angelo and Angeline flew south above Beale Street and landed at the Beale Street entrance of the FedEx Forum.

Outside, the military and law enforcement agencies had concrete barricades surrounding the FedEx Forum and the Memphis Rock N' Soul Museum.

Tanks, police cruisers and fire trucks sat outside the barricades as armed servicemen kept watch behind, on top and in front of the vehicles.

The heroes were greeted with cheers and applause as a group of nurses and doctors rushed out of the lobby with a stretcher for Jeff.

"Sgt. Cheshier-Reed told us you two were bringing someone who was in very bad shape," a female doctor said.

"His name is Jeff," Angelo said as he placed Jeff on the stretcher.

"We'll do everything we can for him and we'll keep you updated," the doctor said as she and her group strapped Jeff in and gave him oxygen.

"You keep fighting, Jeff," Angeline said as she kissed his forehead. You have many more battles to fight."

Jeff slowly moved his right hand and made a thumbs up sign as he was taken inside the Forum.

Angeline and Angelo smiled.

"That's a good sign," Angeline said.

"He's strong," Angelo said. "He'll make it."

Sirens blasted through the air and panic filled everyone's hearts, including Angelo's and Angeline's.

"WE'VE GOT INCOMING!" a soldier shouted as he pointed north.

S.O.L.A.D.™: It's Just the Beginning

Angelo and Angeline flew up into the air and saw hundreds of demon soldiers marching down South Third Street, heading straight for the Forum.

The injured people and medical staff rushed into the Forum as the soldiers and law enforcement officers aimed their weapons toward the advancing demon army.

Angeline rolled her eyes and sighed as Angelo cracked his knuckles and stretched.

"We're gonna need help," Angeline said.

"Yep," Angelo said as he looked at the demon army and back at the soldiers and law enforcement officers. "And it's right behind us."

Angelo pulled a purity bomb from one of his pouches and squeezed it in the palm of his hand. "I'm just going to need a few minutes to make some purity bombs into some…"

Angelo opened his hand and there sat a purity bomb in the shape of a bullet.

"Purity bullets?" Angeline asked as she stared at the bullet.

"Yep," Angelo said.

"That isn't the first time you've done that, is it?"

"No," Angelo said. "We don't have time to go into it now, but I taught myself how to do it when I left the Village of Memphis… when you were searching for me."

Angeline murmured something and even Angelo's super hearing was unable to pick it up. He wanted to ask her to repeat what she had said, but he knew he had just opened an old wound and possibly endangered the relationship that seemed to be repairing.

"I'm sorry," Angelo said. "I didn't mean to make you angry again."

Angeline motioned for Angelo to stop talking. "It's okay. We have an army to destroy. I'll create force fields along the streets that intersect with Third Street and hopefully buy you enough time to make as many different types of purity bullets as you can."

"Are you sure you are ready to start making force fields again?" Angelo asked.

"Do I really have a choice?" Angeline asked. "Besides, these force fields won't be as big or require as much power to keep up."

Angeline looked back at the advancing demon army.

"At least I hope it doesn't."

Tyrone Tony Reed Jr.

15

Last Ditch Efforts

It took Angeline less than a minute to create four, thick, 13-feet tall, purple force fields at the intersections of South Third Street and Gayoso Avenue; South Third Street and Peabody Place; South Third Street and Beale Street and South Third Street and the alley that ran along the north side of the FedEx Forum.

"I'm ready," Angeline said to Angelo, who was passing out large stacks of purity bullets he had created for the different firearms that the law enforcement officers and soldiers had.

"Me too," Angelo said as he handed out his last stack of purity bombs and ran to Angeline's side. "How're you and those force fields holding up?"

Angeline held her hands out toward her force fields and every once and a while, her hands shook.

Angelo looked down the street and saw the demon soldiers pounding on the force field at the intersection of South Third Street and Gayoso Avenue.

"We're hanging in there," Angeline said. "How are things back there?"

"They're ready," Angelo said as he pulled out his Sword of Faith and split it into two swords. "Are you?"

Angeline's Sais of Faith floated out of their holsters and into her awaiting hands.

"As ready as I'll ever be," Angeline said. "But, I hope this is the last demon army we have to defeat."

"I wouldn't bank on that," Angelo said. "The Demon Master is trying to wear us down so we won't have the strength to fight him."

"Well, if that was his plan, it has definitely worked," Angeline said as she watched the demon soldiers crack and seconds later, burst through her first force field. "At times, I feel like my legs…my entire body might give out."

"If they do, find enough strength to get out of here and hide somewhere safe," Angelo said.

"I'm not going to leave you here alone," Angeline said as they watched the demon soldiers destroy the force field at the intersection of South Third Street and Peabody Place.

"I know," Angelo said. "I've got you and God on my side and about hundred law enforcement officers backing us up."

Angeline gave Angelo a weak smile. "Sorry. I'm almost too tired to smile."

"A weak one is better than not getting anything," Angelo said as the force field at the intersection of Beale Street and South Third Street collapsed.

"GET READY, EVERYONE!" Angelo shouted as the demon soldiers reached the last force field and pounded on it with their fists and weapons.

Angelo got into a lunging position and held his swords toward the advancing demon army.

The soldiers and law enforcement officers behind Angelo and Angeline aimed their weapons at the demon army and prepared to fire.

Angelo nodded at Angeline, signaling to her to drop the force field. But, instead of dropping it, Angeline twirled around at super speed and used her speed to slam the force field into the first three lines of the demon army like a battling ram. Those three lines were instantly destroyed and burst into ashes.

Angelo ran into the demon soldiers at super speed and sliced through them with complete abandonment. His legs buckled every other minute and he paused for a few seconds before continuing his onslaught.

Angeline was a few feet behind him, using her sais to telekinetically attack the demon soldiers while she shot purity arrows with her bow.

As the two heroes fought, a barrage of purity bullets whizzed past them and struck the demon soldiers around them.

One by one, sometimes two by two, the demon soldiers burst into flames and burned into ashes.

"We're doing it," Angeline said into her earpiece,

"Yep," Angelo said as he continued to fight and periodically watch large groups of demon soldiers burst into ashes. "Just keep them from getting to our backup and the people inside the Forum."

Angelo and Angeline moved their attack up South Third Street. As they did, the soldiers and law enforcement officers advanced several feet behind them, continuing to give the heroes cover fire.

Angeline was so excited about having decimated over half of the demon army that she didn't notice a large demon soldier perched on the rooftop of a nearby building.

The demon soldier had a large battle-axe in his hands and waited for some small demon soldiers to lead Angeline over to the building.

Angeline fired three arrows into the three demon soldiers and they instantly ignited. She turned to fight several more demon soldiers, which had surrounded her and were forcing her closer to the building.

Angelo saw Angeline through the demon soldiers and looked up to the rooftop, spotting the large demon soldier preparing to leap off the rooftop and attack Angeline.

Angelo connected his swords together at their hilts, forming a lance, and hurled it toward the demon soldier on the rooftop.

Angeline attacked the demon soldiers that had her surrounded and Angelo threw out a large amount of purity bombs on the demon soldiers around him as he flew into the air and headed toward the demon soldier on the rooftop.

The demon soldier was surprised when Angelo's lance struck his battle-axe and destroyed it. The impact caused the demon soldier to stumble back from the ledge and seconds later, Angelo flew into him at super speed.

"GET OFF ME," the demon soldier screamed as he swatted Angelo across the other side of the rooftop. "YOU ARE NOT WORTHY TO TOUCH ME!"

The demon soldier clapped his hands and slowly moved them away from each other, revealing a new, giant battle-axe forming before him.

"MY MASTER WILL REWARD ME HANDSOMELY WHEN I DELIVER YOUR HEAD TO HIM," the demon soldier said.

Angelo held his right hand in the air and his lance flew to him. Angelo squeezed the hilt and the lance turned back into one large sword.

"If you want this head," Angelo said, "come and get it."

The demon soldier gripped his battle-axe tightly and raced toward Angelo. When he was a few feet away from Angelo, he swung his battle-axe downward.

Angelo dodged the swing at super speed and slashed the demon soldier on the left side of his body.

The demon soldier gritted its teeth and swung his battle-axe horizontally at Angelo.

Angelo slid under the battle-axe and at super speed, placed several purity bombs onto the demon soldier's boots before diving between the demon soldier's legs.

A second later, the purity bombs exploded, making the demon soldier fall onto his knees as his legs burst into flames.

"YOU'LL NEVER DEFEAT OUR MASTER," the demon soldier said as he tried to put the flames out.

Angelo walked back to the edge of the rooftop and floated off of it.

"We will," Angelo said. "Just like we are defeating each one of you."

The demon soldier grabbed his battle-axe and stood up on his disintegrating legs. He lifted the battle-axe over his head with both hands and prepared to throw it into Angelo's back.

Just before the demon soldier could let his battle-axe fly, a sniper from on top of the FedEx Forum fired several rounds into the demon soldier's head.

Angelo turned around to see the demon soldier's body burst into flames and the battle-axe fall to the rooftop.

As the ashes of the demon soldier accumulated, Angelo turned, saluted the sniper and jumped back into the fight against the remaining demon soldiers.

"You okay?" Angeline asked as she floated over to Angelo.

"Yeah," Angelo said as his shield appeared before him. He swung it hard through the demon soldiers in front of him and willed it to come back to him. The demon soldiers burst into flames and into ashes seconds later.

"I know which superhero you got that move from," Angeline said.

Angelo smiled but not for long as he spotted a group of flying demon soldiers heading toward the FedEx Forum from the east.

Angeline saw it also.

"Go," Angeline said. "There are only about a hundred demon soldiers left. Go stop them. The fellas and I got this."

Angelo readied himself to fly into the air when his super hearing picked up the flying demon soldiers' scattered thoughts.

Distract the heroes… especially Angelo…injure them if you can… but do not kill them. The words continued to repeat in their minds as they got closer and closer to the Forum.

"Did you hear that?" Angelo asked Angeline.

"Hear what?"

"Those flying demon soldiers, and probably the ones we've been fighting, are distracting us," Angelo said.

"From what?" Angeline asked.

"That's what we need to find out," Angelo said.

The soldiers and law enforcement officers rushed past Angelo and Angeline and shot the remaining demon soldiers.

The snipers on the FedEx Forum rooftop took out the flying demon soldiers.

Cheers once again erupted among the soldiers, law enforcement officers and the people they had protected.

Angelo and Angeline floated into the air and looked around the city.

"Where is he?" Angelo asked. "What is the Demon Master doing?"

"Kristopher, I'm worried," Kandace Edwards said as she watched the news and continued redialing her son Kevin's cell phone number. "I keep getting a stupid message about how the lines are all busy."

Kristopher Edwards tried not to look worried, but he was very concerned about his son and his daughter Patricia, who had been scheduled to land in Memphis hours ago.

"Honey, all we can do is pray right now that Kevin, Juanita and Patricia are safe and away from the monsters," Kristopher said as he hugged his wife. "The news anchors told everyone to stay in their homes and the military isn't allowing anyone into the downtown area."

"I don't care," Kandace said as she grabbed her keys off the kitchen counter. "We are going to find our kids."

The doorbell rang as Kandace walked to the front door.

"Maybe that's them," Kristopher said as he ran to the door and opened it.

There stood a tall, hooded man in a black ceremonial robe with purple and black trimming.

"Can we help you sir?" Kristopher asked.

"Yes…you can…mother and father," the man said as his eyes glowed orange.

Tyrone Tony Reed Jr.

16

Family Reunion

"Excuse me sir, but you must be mistaken," Kristopher said. He tried to push the man out of the doorway, but the man wouldn't budge.

"You're a pretty strong fella," Kristopher said as he continued to try to push the man back outside. "Please leave before I call the police."

The man laughed as Kristopher's body jerked back, flew into the air and slammed against the ceiling.

"I think the police are preoccupied at the moment," the man said as his eyes glowed orange.

"KRIS!" Kandace screamed as she reached for her husband. "LET HIM GO, DEMON!"

Kandace lunged at the man to punch him in the head, but before she could land the punch, she found herself unable to move.

"That's no way for a mother to treat her long lost child," the man said as he telekinetically forced Kandace and Kris to sit down on the sofa.

Even though the tone of the man's voice was gruff and full of anger, Kandace heard something so familiar to her.

"Kevin?" Kandace asked, shocked that she had even formed her lips to say her son's name.

"I'M NOT KEVIN!" the man screamed as he removed his hood, revealing an older, scarred and demonic-looking man, who looked like an older version of Kevin. "I'm the other one. The one you thought died during delivery."

"Brian?" Kandace said. "That can't be possible."

"It is, Mother," the man said. "My brother, the Demon Master, found me years after my abduction and replacement, but not before you two were killed."

"Demon Master?" Kris asked. "Are you telling us that Kevin is a…master of demons and you…What are you?"

The man smiled, showcasing two rows of very sharp, abnormally long teeth as his mouth seemed to grow longer to accommodate his teeth. "I am the Demon Maestro."

Kris laughed. "Yeah, right. There's no way you are who you say you are. I don't know what kind of sick joke you are trying to pull, but there's no way my sons, even though they were born at midnight on Halloween, would ever become monsters like you and your brother."

Kris' laughter angered the Demon Maestro, so much so that he pulled out a long black sword and stopped short of cutting into Kris' neck.

"STOP!!!" Kandace screamed. "Please, don't kill him."

Tears streamed down Kandace's face as she motioned for the Demon Maestro to lower his sword.

"I'm…glad that you are alive," Kandace said. "You do not know how many nights I cried over losing you. I had planned this life of having happy, healthy twin boys and then, after I was told you had died during childbirth…it was so hard."

The Demon Maestro lowered his sword and stepped back. He relaxed his shoulders and appeared to soften at Kandace's words.

"And…is it still hard now?" the Demon Maestro asked. "How often do you think of me or mention me?"

Kandace wept.

"Yes, it's still hard…because I didn't get to raise my baby," Kandace said as Kris tried to console her. "We might not…talk about you like we once did, but we've never forgotten about you. I think of you every time I look into Kevin's eyes."

Kandace wiped her eyes. "Where is…your brother?"

The Demon Maestro grew angry again and lifted up his sword.

"Your stupid, wretched son killed him...the king of my world," the Demon Maestro said. "That's why I'm here. That's why I attacked this city. My brother was the only family I had and your son came to our world and took him away from me. So, I've come to take the two of you away from him."

"What are you talking about?" Kris asked. "Are you saying our son has been to another world? You're delusional."

The Demon Maestro grabbed Kris up by his shirt with one hand and pointed his sword to the flat-screen television with his other hand.

"Really," the Demon Maestro said. "You see demons on your television set and two annoying super beings fighting, in vain, against them and you say I'm delusional."

Kandace stood up and placed her hand on the Demon Maestro's chest.

"I believe you," Kandace said. "I don't know how it's possible, but I do."

The Demon Maestro threw Kris onto the sofa and looked into Kandace's eyes.

"I can see the hurt and anger in your eyes," Kandace said. "I don't know what happened to you and your brother to make you this way, but it's not too late to change. I'll pray for you and I'll do everything I can to help you. You can be a part of this family."

The Demon Maestro smacked Kandace back to the sofa and scoffed at her.

Kris tried to get up to attack the Demon Maestro, but Kandace held him back.

Kandace slowly reached into her pocket and pulled out her flip phone. She felt for the tiny raised bubble on the "5" on the keypad and moved her finger diagonally to the "3". She pressed it long and hard and was thankful that she didn't have the keypad tone on.

The words, "Kevin-Son", popped up as she speed-dialed Kevin.

"I'm not here for redemption, woman," the Demon Maestro said. "I'm way past that. I'm here for revenge. I'm here to kill your son and his little girlfriend, but only after I kill the two of you in front of them."

"See anything?" Angeline asked through her earpiece.

"Nothing but a few demon soldiers and demon dogs, which I'm about to take care of," Angelo said as he swooped out of the sky and landed in front of the National Civil Rights Museum. "Whatever the Demon Master is planning, I don't see a specific place that he is attacking."

Angelo jammed handfuls of purity bombs into the mouths of the demon dogs at super speed. He quickly turned his attention to the group of demon soldiers attempting to break into the museum to eat the people who had ran inside to hide.

"Excuse me," Angelo said. "The museum is open for people, not hell spawns."

The demon soldiers turned around and ran toward Angelo, who pulled his sword out and quickly defeated the five demon soldiers.

S.O.L.A.D.™: It's Just the Beginning

"How's Jeff?" Angelo asked.

"I don't know," Angeline said as she tried to move around the Forum. It was difficult because the people inside were crowding her, asking her to help them or thanking her for saving their lives. "I can't get through to find him and I'm afraid if I go inside any further, people might start trampling each other to get to me."

Angeline walked out of the front doors of the Forum and the soldiers and law enforcement tried to make the people back away from her.

"Thanks, guys," Angeline said as she flew high into the air and out of sight.

She landed on the rooftop of the Orpheum Theatre and looked around at the damage caused by the battle that occurred in the streets below hours earlier.

"Boy, the city is going to need a lot of renovations and repairs when this is over," Angeline said.

"Yep," Angelo said as he landed next to her. "I just hope we aren't blamed for it."

"Even if we are, we did the best we could to keep the damage in downtown and to keep it from spilling into residential areas."

Angelo looked around at the plumes of smoke and ashes blowing into the air across the city.

"We don't know that for sure," Angelo said. "We have no way of knowing how many demons got outside of the city."

"Then, once we take care of the Demon Master, we'll find the rest of his demons and take of them too."

"We just have to find their master," Angelo said.

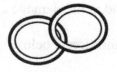

"My brother would've loved to have been a part of this," the Demon Maestro said as he watched the footage streaming from a news chopper being broadcast on television. "This is what we lived for when we first took over our world all those years ago."

"So, you're from the future?" Kris asked.

"Does it matter?" the Demon Maestro asked. "You won't be alive in few minutes to even care."

"Our sons wouldn't be doing what you are doing or what you claimed you did in the past or whatever time or world you're from," Kandace said as she continued to speed dial Kevin over and over again.

"But, we did, Mother," the Demon Maestro said. "And we did it all in loving memory of the two of you."

"We wouldn't have asked you two to do something like that, especially not for us," Kris said.

"But, my brother loved his dear old parents and sister so much, that when they were murdered, by the very people he had rescued time and time again, he decided that the situation didn't call for him to be a hero anymore," the Demon Maestro said. "My brother decided that it was time to punish the people of our world. After all, he had spent many years of his life protecting them and saving them and how did they show their appreciation?"

The Demon Maestro paused as he turned from the television and faced Kris and Kandace.

"First, this weak little preacher named Jerry Wiseman calls my brother and his family 'demons' and exposes their secret identities on national and international television. Then he blames them for several bombings."

The Demon Maestro laughed. "My brother was okay with that and ready to prove the accusations of terrorism false. That is until the two of you and our sister were murdered in retaliation for the bombings. When that happened…my brother truly realized his purpose, to be ruler of the maggots he had protected and to make sure no one ever hurt him or his family again."

"So you and your brother made a deal with the devil?" Kandace asked.

"No, Mom, we became gods and waged war against the very being who gave us these powers and turned on us."

"Sweetheart," Kandace said, "God didn't turn His back on the two of you. You turned your back on Him. Didn't you and Kevin even think about the fact that we...our future selves...your parents...were safe in Heaven, despite the violent way you claimed we...they...died?"

"I personally didn't care, especially since I wasn't raised by the two of you," the Demon Maestro said. "But, Kevin...poor Kevin, he couldn't let it go and it put him at odds with his treacherous wife and his ungrateful children. He couldn't have anyone with similar powers trying to betray him, so...he killed them."

Kandace gasped and the Demon Maestro broke into laughter.

"What's the matter, Mommy?" the Demon Maestro asked. "Too much to handle? Too devastating to think about?"

"That's enough," Kris said as he stood up and got in the Demon Maestro's face. "We don't want to hear anymore of your lies."

"They're not lies," the Demon Maestro said. "They're fact. They're my history."

"So, why tell us all of this if you're just going to kill us?" Kandace asked. "Won't doing that change your past and our future?"

The Demon Maestro grinned as he pushed Kris back on the sofa and pressed the blade of his sword next to Kris' throat.

"I really don't care," the Demon Maestro said. "I'm doing this because I enjoy making people miserable before I kill them. My brother was straight to the point about killing, but, I've always had a flair for torture, mentally and physically."

The Demon Maestro made a quick cut on the side of Kris' neck, causing Kris to slap his hand against the wound.

"Please stop," Kandace said as she checked Kris' neck. "You don't have to do this. We can talk this out."

"I'm sure you would like that, Mom, so you can continue stalling and keep trying to contact your boy," the Demon Maestro said as he telekinetically floated Kandace's flip phone from her side and made it explode. "You don't have to call him. I will."

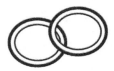

"This is driving me crazy," Angelo said as he and Angeline flew low between buildings.

Periodically, they would land and destroy regular demons, demon soldiers and demon dogs before flying back into the air and continuing their search for the Demon Master.

"It just doesn't make any sense," Angelo said.

"What doesn't?" Angeline said.

"Any of it," Angelo said. "On Dark Earth, the Demon Master told me he wanted to make me like him."

"Why and how did he think that he could do that?" Angeline asked.

"He said we were similar and that I reminded him of himself when he was younger."

Angeline looked at Angelo's face and saw his lip quiver. She knew that it was a response to stress and had a strong feeling that it was not because of the current battle but from something that happened on Dark Earth.

"There's something you're not telling me about your fight with the Demon Master, isn't there?"

Angelo wouldn't allow himself to look at Angeline. *How can I tell her that not only is that monster my future self, but that I kill her and our kids in the future so that I can take over our world?*

"Angelo, do you hear me?' Angeline asked.

Angelo was so lost in thought that he nearly sideswiped a building, but Angeline grabbed his arm and flew him away from it.

"KEVIN!" Angeline screamed.

Hearing his real name caused Angelo to regain his train of thought and come back to the conversation.

"I'm...okay," Angelo said. "I was just thinking..."

"About lying to me some more?"

"No..."

"Kevin, I've known you since we were little and I can tell when you are hiding something and when you are lying to me. So tell me what it is."

Angelo knew Angeline was becoming angry with him and he didn't want that. The time that they had spent on Dark Earth seemed to hint at the possibility of the two of them reuniting and forging a stronger, lasting relationship with each other. But, the images of the dark future that would one day unfold terrified Kevin and he refused to become the monster he thought he had destroyed on Dark Earth.

"I'll tell you once this is over," Angelo said as he forced a smile on his face.

"You can save that fake smile," Angeline said as she flew ahead of Angelo. "And you can save that lie too."

Angelo was about to apologize when he got an intense headache and began flying closer to the street.

Angeline turned back and saw Angelo's descent and saw him holding his head while gritting his teeth.

"What's wrong?"

"I...don't...know..." Angelo said as Angeline grabbed his arm and helped him land on the street below.

Angelo fell to his knees and screamed loudly, causing the windows in the buildings around him to shatter.

Angeline created a force field around her and Angelo as the glass showered onto them.

She massaged her ears and thanked God for the gift of super healing as her eardrums healed after being burst by Angelo's scream.

"What's going on?" Angeline asked Angelo again.

"Something...is...torturing...me," Angelo said as he lied on the ground in a fetal position.

Angeline knelt beside him and gently placed her hands on his head. Her hands glowed white and the white energy flowed to Angelo's head, alleviating the pain.

Good thing you're there with him, girl, a gruff voice said to the heroes telepathically. *I was never good at the telepathy thing. I'm more of a hands-on master of demons.*

"It's him," Angeline said as she helped Angelo stand.

"It doesn't sound like him," Angelo said. "The Demon Master's been inside my head before, for way too long, and he didn't sound like that. This person sounds…twisted… like he gets pleasure from tormenting others."

I needed to get your attention, the Demon Maestro continued, unaware of the heroes' verbal conversation. *I know you are ready to end this, boy, and I am too.*

So...Come home now. Our parents are waiting to say goodbye to you. But, you better hurry or they won't get the chance.

Tyrone Tony Reed Jr.

17

"Do Great Things"

"**O**h, this is gonna be a great fight," the Demon Maestro said before smiling at Kris and Kandace. "I can hear your son breaking the sound barrier now. He'll be here in about six seconds."

The Demon Maestro raised his sword over his head. "That's just enough time for him to fly in here and see me kill the two of you with one stroke."

The wall behind the Demon Maestro exploded as Angelo flew through it, tackled the Demon Maestro and slammed him through the wall of the kitchen.

Angeline flew through the hole a few seconds later and helped Kris and Kandace off the couch.

"Come on, Mr. and Mrs. Edwards," Angeline said as she picked them up and flew out of the hole and into the front yard. She laid them beside a bush a few feet away from their house. "Are you two okay?"

Kris and Kandace both looked Angeline over twice before they both asked in unison, "Juanita?"

Angeline nodded. "But, when I look like this, I'm Angeline."

The three of them looked back through the hole in the front wall of the house and saw Angelo punching and kicking the Demon Maestro through the kitchen.

"And that's...Kevin?" Kandace asked.

"Yes," Angeline said. "It's a long story, but we need to deal with the Demon Master first."

"That's not the Demon Master," Kandace said. "He says he's our son...Kevin's twin brother."

"What?" Angeline asked. "That's not possible. Kevin told me his twin died during childbirth."

"It…he…claims he is our son, just older and that he wants revenge on Kevin for killing his twin brother," Kris said.

"That means…" Angeline didn't want to finish the statement, but she felt she had to say it out loud so that she could confirm that it was real. "The Demon Master...was an older Kevin."

Angeline replayed her memories of Dark Earth and all that she and Kevin had experienced there.

"All that time," Angeline said, "we were in the future…our future…"

"Juanita…Angeline," Kandace said. "You need to focus...on the present."

"Yes, like right now," Kris said as he helped Kandace up and pointed to the street. "There are monsters on our street now."

Angeline turned around to see about 50 demon soldiers, ready for battle.

Angeline created a force field around Kris and Kandace, who gasped as they were surrounded by it and carried high into the air.

"Don't worry," Angeline said as she pulled out her sais. "It'll protect you and keep you safe until this is over."

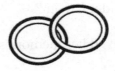

Angelo grabbed the Demon Maestro's head and slammed it through the kitchen wall. The wall crumbled as the rest of the Demon Maestro's body went through the wall and he landed in the backyard.

"You held my parents hostage," Angelo said as he kicked the Demon Maestro further into the backyard. "You attacked them and you tried to kill them too."

Angelo ran at super speed and yanked the Demon Maestro off the ground. He quickly delivered two punches and a roundhouse kick to the Demon Maestro's face. The impact of the blows flung the Demon Maestro through a large tree.

Angelo was over the Demon Maestro before he had time to react. Angelo punched him into the ground, over and over again, with such force, that the ground shook violently for miles.

"YOU SHOULDN'T HAVE COME TO MY WORLD!" Angelo shouted. "YOU SHOULDN'T HAVE MESSED WITH MY PARENTS!"

The Demon Maestro caught the next punch and kicked Angelo out of the hole that had been created by Angelo's powerful punches.

Angelo crashed into the shed behind his house and struggled to get up.

"AND YOU SHOULDN'T HAVE KILLED MY BROTHER," the Demon Maestro said as he hovered high above Angelo.

"Your brother?" Angelo said. "Then…that means…"

"Yes," the Demon Maestro said as he dropped down on Angelo at super speed, driving him eight feet into the ground. The Demon Maestro floated out of the hole and landed on the ground. "It means you're dead and your world is mine."

Kris and Kandace watched as Angeline moved at super speed, running through the crowd of demon soldiers and fighting them.

"Wow, she's moving so fast that at times, I can't even see her," Kris said.

"I still can't believe all this is happening," Kandace said as she maneuvered herself over Kris so she could see the backyard. "We've met an evil, future or alternate world version of a son we thought was dead and now we are watching our other son and his ex-girlfriend fight demons with their super powers."

"At least they are winning," Kris said. "And they won't be exes for long."

"I hope they do," Kandace said.

Kris took his eyes off Angeline's fight to look into the eyes of his wife.

"You can't mean that," Kris said. "You, I, Kevin and Juanita know the two of them are meant to be together. God created the two of them to do great things in this world, which they are doing right before our very eyes. Imagine what they are going to do together...as a couple, a family, with their children."

"I don't have to imagine," Kandace said. "The Demon Maestro...our future son...has already told us what their future will be and I don't want it to happen."

Kris scoffed at his wife.

"I can't believe you believe that monster's words," Kris said. "You and I raised Kevin to be better than that Demon Master the Demon Maestro claims Kevin will become. We raised our son to do what's right and we taught him that when he does what is right, right will always follow him."

"I know, Kris, but…"

"No," Kris said. "There are no 'buts'. No matter what the situation is, our son will do what's right. We've seen him do that all his life and the whole world has seen it today on their television sets, cell phones and computer screens. Our son is no demon master. Our son is a hero."

Angelo had heard every word his parents had said, especially his dad's last sentences.

Our son is no demon master. Our son is a hero. The words replayed over and over in Angelo's mind.

Angelo flew out of the hole at super speed and slammed into the back of the Demon Maestro.

"You really are a stupid boy," the Demon Maestro said as his eyes glowed bright orange. "Now I'm going to set you on fire like you did my brother."

Large fiery beams of energy shot out of the Demon Maestro's eyes as he stared at Angelo.

Angelo's shield appeared and grew in size as the Demon Maestro's fire beams grew stronger and stronger.

"When I finish killing you, I'm going to kill your parents, maybe in the same way mine were killed," the Demon Maestro said. "Then I'm going to make your girlfriend my wife, whether she wants to be or not."

The Demon Maestro laughed.

"But, I'm going to torture her either way," he said.

Angelo was on his knees, struggling against the Demon Maestro's fire beams. But, as he heard the plans the Demon Maestro had for his loved ones, he stood and pushed the fire beams back.

The Demon Maestro willed his fire beams to intensify and even though they did, Angelo continued to advance.

"Stop," the Demon Maestro said as Angelo got closer and closer. "Come on…I was just joking."

Angelo slammed his shield into the Demon Maestro's face, causing the Demon Maestro's fire beams to stop and knocking the Demon Maestro on his back.

The Demon Maestro threw his hands out in front of himself defensively, as if he were about to be struck by Angelo.

"Please…" the Demon Maestro said. "Show mercy. I was…misguided…unjustifiably angry when I was the one doing wrong."

Angelo pulled out his sword.

"I'm not falling for your tricks anymore," Angelo said.

"This is no trick, brother," the Demon Maestro said. "I did all of this for you...or future you...especially after you liberated me from that lab all those years ago. You have no idea how I was tortured by those demons and that scientist."

"Save it," Angelo said as he lifted his sword over his head. "I'm not your brother. I'll never be him."

The Demon Maestro whimpered for a moment, causing Angelo to hesitate delivering a fatal blow. A second later, the Demon Maestro laughed and faded away.

Angelo drove his sword into the ground where the Demon Maestro had been seconds before and screamed in frustration.

"It was worth a shot," the Demon Maestro said reappearing in the sky. "You shouldn't have hesitated. My brother wouldn't have. Now your mommy and daddy are gonna die."

The Demon Maestro turned his head and focused his eyes on Kris and Kandace, who were still floating several feet off the ground inside Angeline's force field.

Fire beams shot from the Demon Maestro's eyes and headed straight for the force field.

If he can do it, so can I, Angelo thought as his eyes glowed white and he took off his shades.

The white energy from his eyes shot out and struck the Demon Maestro in the back, knocking him out of the sky.

The Demon Maestro's fire beams stopped, just inches from destroying Kris, Kandace and the force field they were in.

Angeline finished defeating the demon soldiers just in time to see two white beams of light knock the Demon Maestro out of the sky.

S.O.L.A.D.™: It's Just the Beginning

The Demon Maestro crashed through the roof of the Edwardses' house as Angeline lowered the force field, which held Kris and Kandace, back to the ground.

"Thanks," Kandace said to Angeline as the force field faded away.

"Don't thank me yet," Angeline said as she walked toward the house. "The Demon Maestro's still breathing."

The house exploded as Angeline approached the house from the front and Angelo approached from the back. The blast threw Angelo across the backyard as Angeline created a force field around herself, Kris and Kandace.

"KEVIN!" Kandace screamed.

The Demon Maestro walked out of the fire that engulfed the debris of the house.

"You're all going to die," he said as a large, fiery battle-axe formed in his right hand and he walked toward Angeline.

Angeline used her force field as a battling ram and slammed it over and over again into the Demon Maestro.

The Demon Maestro stumbled backward with each blow, but on the sixth attack, he lifted his battle-axe into the air and sliced through Angeline's force field.

He flew up to her at super speed, grabbed her by the neck and threw her into the driveway.

Piercing pain shot through Angeline's body as she tried to get up.

"Don't bother," the Demon Maestro said as he drove his boot into her back. "I don't think I want to play with you anymore. I think you can die now."

Purity bombs suddenly exploded on the Demon Maestro's back. He turned around and saw Angelo flying above the burning debris.

"Can't put me down so you attack a young lady?" Angelo asked as he landed a few feet away.

The Demon Maestro smiled and threw his battle-axe into the ground. He yanked off his cloak, revealing an all black outfit, with an orange tie, which resembled Angelo's outfit.

"We Edwards boys have nice taste," the Demon Maestro said as he yanked his battle-axe out of the ground. "But, I'm so glad my brother and I changed to darker colors because they make us look so fly."

"Shut up and fight," Angelo said as he pulled out his sword. "This has gone on long enough. Everybody wants to go home and get some shut-eye."

"Ever the jokester, ever the fool," the Demon Maestro said as his battle-axe clanged against Angelo's sword. "I'm going to enjoy killing you in front of them and I will finally have revenge on you for my brother's murder."

"This isn't about your brother," Angelo said as he punched the Demon Maestro hard in the chest and yanked his battle-axe away from him. "It never was. You just wanted your own world to rule."

Angelo laughed, which made the Demon Maestro nervous.

"The Demon Master probably had you tucked away on the other side of Dark Earth," Angelo said. "Gave you a few people to torture to satisfy your bloodlust, but told you never to show yourself. Probably told you it was for your own good."

"He had a big plan and we had to stick to it…so it would be successful," the Demon Maestro said. "He had a great plan."

"Right," Angelo said as he walked up to the Demon Maestro. "How did that work out?"

Kris and Kandace pulled Angeline away from the driveway and behind some bushes.

"Are you alright, Juanita?" Kris asked.

"I'm getting there," Angeline said. "How's Angelo doing?"

"He's doing great," Kris said, making sure to look over to his wife. "Our son is a hero. Always has been. Always will be."

"If you think this is something, wait until you hear about what he did for a year on another planet...or maybe the supposed future," Angeline said. "There were things that changed him...changed us."

Kandace placed her hand on Angeline's. "But, you were there for each other, right? No matter what happened, you did take care of each other?"

Angeline nodded. "In the end, we had each other's backs."

"A year?" Kris said with a puzzled look. "You've only been gone for a couple of hours. Don't tell me there was some magical portal at the library that swept the two of you away to another world?"

Angeline tried not to giggle.

"Mr. Edwards, you always seem to know what's going on," she said.

"Did Kevin or Angelo hurt you?" Kandace asked.

"What?" Angeline was shocked that Kandace had asked that question.

"Kandace," Kris said. "You heard what I said. Don't listen to that monster."

"I just need to know," Kandace said. "I just need to be sure. See, the Demon Maestro said that in his past, our future, Kevin is going to…"

"Shhh, Kandace," Kris said. "I don't care what he said. The future…parallel world or alternate universe…I know our son and you know him too. He's not going to become that monster.'

Kris put his arm on Angeline's shoulder and gave it a light squeeze.

"And if he's ever tempted to, Juanita will be there to steer him away from that temptation," Kris said. "Ain't that right?"

Angeline nodded as she tried to sit up. She winced in pain and Kris and Kandace gently lowered her back to the ground.

"Take it easy," Kandace said.

"I need to help, Angelo," Angeline said.

"Don't worry," Kris said as he watched his son fight the Demon Maestro. "Looks like he has everything under control."

"You think you're hot stuff now, huh, boy?" the Demon Maestro said before coughing up a large amount of blood. "So, go ahead and kill me already."

Angelo raised his sword and prepared to behead the Demon Maestro.

"But, before you do, you need to realize that you are about to kill not only a human being, but the twin brother you never knew."

The Demon Maestro grinned as he sat forward and pointed toward his heart.

Angelo's sword and arm trembled as he hesitated once again.

"Don't have it in you, do you?"

Angelo screamed as he brought the sword down toward the Demon Maestro and punched him in the face.

"Get off my planet and get out of my time," Angelo said.

Angelo passed by the Demon Maestro, heading toward his parents and Angeline. The three smiled as Angelo got closer to them.

"You know, you were right, Angelo," the Demon Maestro said. "You're definitely not my brother. He would have never turned his back on me."

Angelo turned around just as a black sword formed in the Demon Maestro's hand and he ran the sword through Angelo's chest.

"I guess that means becoming a demon master is not in your future," the Demon Maestro said as he placed his left foot on Angelo's chest to pull his sword out of him. "Actually, I'm not sure you were ever going to become him. There are so many universes out there...so many Angelos, Angelines, Demon Masters and Demon Maestros...or at least there use to be before my brother and I came along."

Angelo turned back into Kevin as his lifeless body fell to the ground and his parents and Angeline screamed out his name.

"It's okay," the Demon Maestro said as he knelt and closed Kevin's eyes. He looked up at Kris, Kandace and Angeline as he stood up. "You're next."

Kris stood up and grabbed one of Angeline's arrows from her quiver and took off running toward the Demon Maestro.

"NO, YOU'RE NEXT!" Kris screamed.

A force field suddenly appeared between the Demon Maestro and Kris, stopping Kris in his tracks. The force field spread around the area the Demon Maestro stood in and grew thicker.

As it did, Kris turned around to see Kandace helping Angeline to her feet.

"I'm sorry, Mr. Edwards," Angeline said. "Kevin…would never forgive me if I let something happen to you or Mrs. Edwards."

"What now?" Kandace asked Angeline. "Can you kill him or send him back to his time?"

"I don't know," Angeline said. "But, even when things got really bad on Dark Earth, God always helped Kevin and me make it through."

The Demon Maestro tapped on the inside of the force field and grinned.

"You can't keep me in here forever," he said. "While I wait for your powers to wane, I can go ahead and prepare my trophy."

The Demon Maestro walked over to Kevin's body and stood over it for a few seconds.

"STAY AWAY FROM MY SON!" Kandace screamed as she beat the outside of the force field.

A black machete formed in the Demon Maestro's hand as he knelt, grabbed the back of Kevin's head and pulled it up from the ground.

"Don't worry, mom," the Demon Maestro said. "I'll leave everything else below the neck intact. This isn't my first rodeo."

The Demon Maestro was inches away from placing the blade against Kevin's neck when Kevin's body faded away.

Kris and Kandace sighed.

"Thank you,' Kandace said as she turned to look at Angeline.

"GIVE HIM BACK TO ME!" the Demon Maestro screamed as he pounded angrily on the inside of the force field. "HE'S MINE! HE TOOK AWAY MY CHANCE TO KILL MY BROTHER!"

Tears rolled down Kandace's face as the Demon Maestro's words echoed in her mind.

"You...wanted to...kill...your brother?" Kandace asked. "Why? You said he saved you?"

The Demon Maestro stopped pounding on the force field and stared at Kandace.

"Dear stupid mommy," he said. "While it's true that my brother found me, rescued me from a demented scientist obsessed with cloning, I was reduced to standing in my brother's shadow, not by his side. And when he took over the world, he sent me away so I wouldn't get in his way. In other words...I LOATHED HIM."

Kris grabbed Kandace and walked her away from the force field.

"Sweetheart, don't talk or listen to that monster anymore," Kris said. "The only important thing now is that we have Kevin, right Angeline?"

Angeline shrugged her shoulders.

"I don't have him," Angeline said. "I've never teleported anyone before and I didn't learn how to in the last few minutes."

Kandace looked around as she wiped the tears from her face.

"Then, where did he go?" she asked.

"It's time to get up, my little hero," a young woman said as she touched Kevin's hand. "You've been lying here long enough."

Kevin opened his eyes and saw the same white room of light that he had visited when he was on Dark Earth.

"Who are you?" Kevin asked as he stood up.

"Have you forgot about me already?" the woman asked. "You were just here three weeks ago, at least in your time."

Kevin rubbed his eyes and took a double-take.

"Grandma Isabella?" he asked.

"Yes," she said. "It's me."

"You look younger," Kevin said.

"Yes," she said. "This is my true appearance. I only appeared to you last time as my elderly self so you would readily accept what I needed to say to you."

"And now?"

"Now, Kevin, you have all the time in the world. Or all the time in eternity."

Kevin looked himself over and then back at his grandmother.

"I don't feel anything," Kevin said. He paused for a few seconds and hung his head. "I'm…dead."

Isabella kissed Kevin's forehead and hugged him.

"No, my little hero," she said. "You died, but you now have eternal life through Jesus. All that pain, suffering and heartache from that world is over."

"I know," Kevin said. "I can feel it. I feel peace… joy… love… flowing through me. There's not even a hint of sadness, fear or despair."

"Then you are ready to go to your eternal home?" Isabella asked. "You are ready, aren't you?"

Kevin smiled as the white light behind Isabella opened up and revealed a golden road that had beautiful flowers and trees growing on both sides of it. Kevin could also hear the sound of amazing, singing voices, which echoed through the air, singing praises to God and Jesus.

Further off, he could see people, dressed in immaculate clothing, who all appeared to be at their prime. The people were healthy, happy and glowing in a light that shined all over Heaven.

"Are you ready, Kevin?" Isabella asked again.

The word "yes" was all Kevin wanted to say when he heard the faint screams of a familiar voice coming from underneath the white floor.

"What is it?" Isabella asked.

Kevin concentrated on the screams and recognized them as belonging to Juanita.

"I can hear Juanita," Kevin said. "She's screaming for me."

"Then you have a choice to make," Isabella said. "The reason you can still hear her is because it's not your time to die, but you are being given a choice to come home to Heaven or finish your life on Earth."

"This is what God planned for me all along, isn't it?" Kevin asked. "He wanted me to see what Heaven was like before going back. Why?"

"So you could see and know that what you have been fighting for down there is so much bigger than you, Juanita and the enemies you have had to face."

Isabella said. "This is about the souls of those you are fighting to protect. You have those powers so you can give them a chance to not just live a great life on that planet, but so they can have a wonderful eternal life in Heaven."

"KEVIN, WHERE ARE YOU?!," Kevin heard Juanita scream.

The white, sparkling floor under Kevin opened up.

"I'm coming," Kevin said as he transformed into Angelo.

He looked at his grandmother and smiled.

Isabella stepped back toward the opening to Heaven.

"My little hero, always remember who you are, not who those demons say you will become," Isabella said. "I really wish I could tell you what it all means, but God will reveal it to you and Juanita in due time."

Angelo listened to his grandmother as he watched the Demon Maestro transform into a giant creature and burst out of Angeline's force field. The creature held its hand out over the area where the Edwardses' house had stood and a large hellhole opened.

"I understand, Grandma," Angelo said. "Thank you for all of your help and please thank God for another chance."

Isabella smiled as she watched Angelo pull out his sword.

"Always remember what I told you last time and everything will work out," Isabella said as she watched demons, demon soldiers and demon dogs climb the interior walls of the giant hellhole. "You and Juanita just hold on to God and each other and everything will be okay."

"We will," Angelo said as he jumped through the hole in front of him. "I love you."

"I love you too," Isabella said as she walked into the light of Heaven.

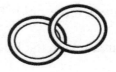

"It doesn't matter where Kevin went," the Demon Maestro said as he walked to the center of the force field that contained him. "You all don't matter and this world doesn't matter either. All that matters is that I have my own world to rule, with no interference."

The Demon Maestro's clothing ripped as his body grew and transformed. He smiled as his body expanded and Angeline's force field cracked.

"But, even though you don't matter, doesn't mean I'm not going to eat the three of you," the Demon Maestro said.

"We have to get out of here," Kandace said.

"You two go ahead," Angeline said as she stretched her hands toward her force field. Every time the force field cracked, she created a new seal over it.

S.O.L.A.D.™: It's Just the Beginning

"Angeline, you can't hold him in that force field forever," Kris said.

"I know, but I can buy the two of you some time," Angeline said. "Get as far away from here as you can."

"TOO LATE!," the Demon Maestro, now a giant, demonic creature, shouted as it broke through the force field and stretched out.

The creature stretched its monstrous hand over the area the Edwardses' house had stood and a giant hellhole opened. Demon dogs, demon soldiers and regular demons climbed the interior walls of the hellhole.

"My loyal subjects are ready to feast on this world," the creature said.

"Go now, Mr. and Mrs. Edwards," Angeline said as her bow appeared in her left hand.

"We can't leave you here alone," Kris said as he grabbed one of Angeline's sais from her belt.

Kandace quickly grabbed the other sai.

"He's right," Kandace said.

"How noble," the creature said as it stood over the hellhole. "You all want to die together? So be it."

The creature opened its mouth wide and bent its body over the hellhole and prepared to chomp down on Angeline, Kris and Kandace when a light burst through the cloudy sky and shined down on the creature.

"What?" the creature said as it turned around and looked up at the opening in the sky.

Out came Angelo, shining bright, holding his sword with both hands. The light forced the demons trying to come up the walls of the hellhole to descend back into the hellhole.

Angelo flew so quickly toward the creature that it didn't realize that it had been decapitated by Angelo's sword until it saw its body reaching for its head.

"Whoa," Kris said as the creature's body and head tumbled into the hellhole.

Angelo, his eyes glowing white behind his shades, floated over the hellhole and light from his body shined straight down into it, burning all the demons to ashes.

A few seconds later, the hellhole closed and Angelo landed.

"KEVIN!" Kandace shouted as Angelo's body continued to glow brighter and brighter.

Angelo held his hand out toward his parents and Angeline, motioning for them to stay where they were.

He said nothing as his body glowed brighter and brighter and the energy surrounding him stretched and expanded, engulfing his parents and Angeline and then the neighborhood.

"What's happening to him?" Kris asked Angeline as he and Kandace covered their eyes.

"I think he's ending this," Angeline said as the light reached downtown. With her super eyesight, Angeline could see the demons burst into ashes as the light made contact with them.

Angeline could feel the light coursing through her body, healing her and strengthening her. But, it wasn't just her that was being healed. She could hear the doctors and patients in the FedEx Forum cheering and clapping as wounds were healed and those who were near death recovered instantly.

"He's healing everyone in the city," Angeline told the Edwards, "and destroying the demons at the same time."

Angelo turned, floated backwards to the hole where the shed had sat and held his hands out toward it.

The shed suddenly came back together, along with the things that had sat inside of it, as the hole in the ground closed.

Angelo then held his hands out over the area where his house had been and the house formed. After about two minutes, the house was complete and better than new.

Angeline watched as Angelo leapt over the house and landed in front of it. He looked up toward the sky and held his hand out toward the barrier.

Energy shot out of Angelo's hands and hit the barrier encasing the city. Moments later, it disappeared.

Angelo walked a few steps toward his parents and Angeline and collapsed.

The light and energy coming from his body faded away moments later and moonlight shined onto the front yard.

When Kris and Kandace opened their eyes, Angelo was gone and Kevin was lying on the ground.

Kris ran to his son and knelt beside him, checking his pulse.

"Is he…?" Kandace asked with tears in her eyes.

"He's alive," Kris said.

A loud snore came from Kevin that made Kris, Kandace and Angeline unexpectedly burst into laughter.

"Typical Kevin," Angeline said. "He saves the world and he's too pooped to celebrate."

"Jeez, he's heavy," Kris said as he tried to lift his son. "When did he get so buff?"

"It's a long story," Angeline said as she picked Kevin up and carried him into the house. "I'll tell you two all about it as soon as I get him to bed."

18

Epilogue: "Learn from the Past..."

Kevin rubbed his eyes as he woke up in his bed.

He sat up, stretched and smiled as the sun shined through his partially opened blinds.

Kevin laid back down and snuggled into his pillow.

"It was just a nightmare," he said softly as he closed his eyes.

The sunlight shining into his room faded away and the sky grew dark. Thunder shook the house, causing Kevin to sit up.

The thunder was followed by a series of flashes of lightning, which temporarily blinded Kevin.

"Whoa," he said as he shut his eyes and waited for his vision to return to normal.

When Kevin opened his eyes a minute later, he saw the Demon Master and the Demon Maestro at the foot of his bed. Demon soldiers surrounded his bed and demon dogs walked around on the ceiling.

"Was it just a nightmare, boy?" the Demon Master and the Demon Maestro asked in unison.

Kevin screamed as the demons tore him apart.

Kevin jumped out of his sleep and leapt out of bed.

It was morning and the sunlight was shining through his partially opened blinds.

He looked around his room, waiting for the demons to attack him at any second. But, after about two minutes, Kevin was sure that they weren't going to appear. Even still, he didn't dare utter the words, "It was just a dream."

Kevin pulled some jeans over his boxers, buttoned up a brown shirt over his white T-shirt and walked out of his room.

He glanced into his parents' room and found their bed unmade, but no one was inside. He checked Patricia's old bedroom, finding the bed unmade and a set of half-opened suitcases laying on it.

Great, Kevin thought. *Tricia made it home safely.*

Kevin walked down the hallway, made his way downstairs and heard the television playing in the living room.

He stood a few feet in front of a large, flat-screen television and watched as Kym Clark, Emmy Award winning news anchor for WMC Action News 5, appeared onscreen and talked about the demon attack on Memphis, the heroes who fought the demons and the aftermath.

"Cleanup efforts are underway in much of downtown Memphis after Saturday's demon attack," Kym said. "The attack was frightening, many witnesses said and the 'angels' they said saved them left them awestruck. We go live to Riverside Drive, where…"

Kevin changed the channel to WREG News Channel 3, where footage, shot by cameraman Ardray Maxwell, showed flying demon soldiers being attacked by Angelo and Angeline in the sky over downtown Memphis.

He changed the channel again, this time to Fox 13 News, where footage, shot by camerawoman Cynthia Perkins, showed Angelo and Angeline fighting demon soldiers alongside law enforcement officers in front of the FedEx Forum.

A few seconds later, Kevin changed the channel to the Local 24 News/CW 30 News broadcast as news anchor Brandon Artiles walked viewers through a timeline of the demonic attack on Memphis.

"What's it like to be a hero?" a female voice asked from the kitchen. "Is it everything you thought it would be?"

Kevin turned around and saw Juanita walking out of the kitchen with two glasses of pink lemonade.

"Not exactly," Kevin said as Juanita handed him a glass. He sipped from it before sitting down on the couch next to her. "I didn't expect to feel this tired."

"Well, someone did show out last night," Juanita said as she nudged Kevin in the ribs.

"Yeah, I kind of remember engulfing the city in light," he said.

"Not just any light," Juanita said. "You healed so many people in the city, including me, with that light."

"I did?"

"Yes," Juanita said. "How did you do it?"

Kevin shrugged his shoulders. "All I remember before doing it was the Demon Maestro running his sword through me. Next thing I know, I'm coming down out of the sky, glowing all over. It was like I was on autopilot."

"Whatever happened, thank God it did," Juanita said. "Your parents and I really thought we were about to die when you disappeared. But, we all made it thanks to you."

"Don't thank me," Kevin said. "Like you said, I thank God because I have no idea how all of that energy came out of me. I was so tired and felt like I was dying before it happened."

Juanita sat her glass on a coaster on an end table.

"That's enough death talk," she said as she grabbed a large newspaper from the coffee table. "Your dad told me to show this to you if you woke up before he, your mom and Tricia got back."

"Where did they go?"

"They went to get breakfast for us and to take some out to the rescue workers and law enforcement officers. Dad and the others are still out their helping get people from under rubble and out of the areas that have been destroyed."

"Too bad my powers didn't repair everything," Kevin said.

"It's okay," Juanita said. "Maybe Angelo and Angeline can help with the repairs, especially since everyone is happy to have them here in the city."

Juanita held up the newspaper, which was a copy of *The Commercial Appeal*, so Kevin could see it.

On the front page was a picture of Angelo and Angeline fighting demons in front of the Art Polo branch of the Memphis Public Library.

The headline of the story read: "Angels vs. Demons." The sub-head read: "Angelo and Angeline save lives and protect the city of Memphis."

"Wow," Kevin said as he looked at the double byline that read "Special report, photos and online videos by Neil and Jennifer Cole."

"Exactly," Juanita said. "S.O.L.A.D. is about to be internationally known, if they aren't already. That couple we met outside the library really did an excellent job writing about what happened. In fact, Robin Meade interviewed them this morning on 'Morning Express'."

"Robinnnnn Meadeeeee," Kevin said.

Juanita smacked him in the back of the head.

"Stop drooling," Juanita said.

"She just looks like she could play Lois Lane in a Superman movie, that's all," Kevin said. "And she seems so nice."

Juanita rolled her eyes. "Anyway, we were also mentioned in the online editions of *The Teen Appeal, The Daily Helmsman, The Memphis Flyer, The Daily News, Memphis Magazine, La Prensa Latina, R.S.V.P. Memphis, The New Tri-State Defender, The Memphis Downtowner and Mediaverse.*"

Kevin grinned at Juanita as he sat the newspaper back on the coffee table.

"We did good, didn't we?" he asked Juanita.

"Yep," Juanita said as she scrolled through her social media feed on her smartphone. "*The Franklin* in Franklin, Indiana, *The West Tennessee Examiner, The Jackson Sun and WBBJ* in Jackson, Tennessee, and *The Tennessean* in Nashville and *The Los Angeles Times' Hero Complex* also had articles online about S.O.L.A.D."

Juanita turned her phone off and sat it on the table.

"Wiseman J would've been proud,." she said.

Kevin's smile faded.

"I almost forgot about…that," Kevin said. "I feel creepy now for being excited about all the news coverage celebrating us as heroes."

"Well, get ready to be creeped out even further, " Juanita said. "After you transformed from Angelo into Kevin and passed out, I carried you in the house and left a few minutes later. I went back to the FedEx Forum and looked for Jeff."

"He's…gone?" Kevin asked.

"Yes, but not in the 'he's dead' way," Juanita said. "In fact, the doctors told me…I mean…told Angeline, that Jeff was out of the danger zone and was set to make a full recovery when a being of white light appeared and picked Jeff up."

"What? Who was it?"

"The doctors didn't know, but they said they could see Jeff's wounds heal instantly as he and the being of white light floated above them and vanished."

"Maybe it was me, Nita. Maybe I did it."

Juanita shook her head.

"It couldn't have been you," she said. "The doctors said it happened a few minutes after we left the FedEx Forum."

"Then we need to go and find him," Kevin said as he scooted to the edge of the couch.

Juanita gently pushed him back and Kevin complied.

"I looked for them for hours and I didn't find anything," Juanita said. "Then…I looked for Wiseman J's body…and it was gone also, along with Jeff's duffel bags and weapons. Jeff hasn't tried to contact me and no new portals have opened."

Kevin drummed his left hand on his left thigh.

"Maybe the being of white light took them back home to Dark Earth," Kevin said.

Juanita shrugged.

"Unless you know how to make portals, all we can do is pray that Jeff is safe," she said.

"Yeah," Kevin said. "You're right."

Kevin looked back at the television as a news ticker on CNN read: "Angelic beings called Angelo and Angeline saved countless lives in Memphis, Tenn. Saturday during a demon attack. The beings said they are called 'Soldiers of Light Against Darkness' or 'S.O.L.A.D.', according to an interview by Jennifer Cole and her husband Neil Cole, who were touring Memphis when the attack occurred."

Photos of Angelo and Angeline in battle, shot by the Coles and Memphis photographer Justin Alan Shaw, were displayed on television.

"I don't think we're the only ones who are going to be famous," Kevin said as he gently squeezed Juanita's hand.

Before Juanita could respond, the ticker on the television screen froze and so did the news anchor.

"Stupid cable," Kevin said as he tried to change the channel.

The channel would not change and the light would not glow on the TV remote as Kevin mashed the buttons.

"It was working fine just a minute ago," Kevin said. "Maybe the batteries died."

"I don't think so," Juanita said as she pointed to a grandfather clock across the room. "It's stopped ticking and so has my watch."

A gust of wind blew from behind Kevin and Juanita, which caused them to stand up and watch as a large blue portal opened up a few feet behind the couch.

"Maybe it's Jeff," Juanita said.

"I don't think so," Kevin said as he and Juanita watched two teenagers, a boy and a girl, step out of the portal and into the living room.

They looked similar to Angelo and Angeline, but they wore different color clothing and they carried different weapons.

The boy was handsome, with short black hair and brown eyes hidden behind slender orange shades. He wore an orange, buttoned vest over a glowing white short-sleeve shirt and white jeans. He also wore an orange tie, orange gloves, an orange belt and orange boots.

He had two orange-handled sais attached to his white belt and an orange quiver, filled with arrows and a crossbow, strapped to his back. He also wore a glowing orange ring on his left ring finger.

The girl wore a purple headband, which kept her long brown hair out of her beautiful face.

Her eyes shimmered purple, which was the color of her sleeveless pantsuit. Her blouse was worn over a tight, white shirt that extended from her collarbone down to her elbows and her waistline.

A white belt with large pouches ran around her waist and a white, double sheath, which held her purple-handled katanas, was strapped to her back.

She wore purple boots and a glowing purple ring shimmered on her left ring finger.

"Who are you?" Juanita asked.

"Isn't it obvious?" asked the boy.

The girl slapped him in the back of the head.

"Of course it isn't," the girl said. "This is the past. They haven't had us yet."

"Or the other five brats that followed us," the boy said.

"Wait…what?" Kevin said.

"I'm sorry for my brother's inability to answer your question correctly," the girl said. "My name is Angelica and his name is Angel Boy. We're members of S.O.L.A.D…"

"Actually, it's A.B. for short," Angel Boy interrupted. "But in two more years, when I turn 18, I'm changing my code name to Angel Man or something cooler and not gonna let my older, by a year and a few months, sister call me Angel Boy ever again."

"Cuz that's important," Angelica said as she stared sternly at her brother. "As I was saying, we are members of S.O.L.A.D. But, our real names are Constance Denise Edwards and Brian Larry Edwards."

"We're your children…from the future," Angel Boy said.

Juanita and Kevin both sat down on the couch at the same time.

Angelica and Angel Boy ran to the front of the couch and checked on their parents, who were clearly in shock.

"Are you okay?" Angelica asked them.

"We've got to be dreaming, because there is no way I'm having seven kids," Juanita said.

"It's not a dream, Mom," Angel Boy said.

"Uncle Jeff said this would happen," Angelica said. "That's why he was reluctant to let us come to the past."

"Wait…Uncle Jeff?" Kevin asked. "You know Jeff? He's all right?"

"Of course he is, Dad," Angelica said. "He comes to our world every month for barbecue and movies."

"If Jeff is okay and, from what I'm hearing, Kevin and I are happily married and have a huge family in the future, why are you two here?" Juanita asked.

Angelica lowered her head as she closed her eyes.

"Because, we can't find the two of you...your future selves," she said. "I used all of my powers to try and find you two and the portal I created led us here...to the past."

"Apparently, you two are the only ones who can help us find...well...the two of you," Angel Boy said. "Your future selves."

"I know this is a lot to take in, especially after what the two of you just went through," Angelica said. "You two always talked about this day when we were growing up."

Kevin and Juanita looked at Angelica and Angel Boy and then pinched each other.

"We aren't dreaming, are we?" Juanita and Kevin asked in unison.

"Nope," Angel Boy said.

Angelica pushed back the coffee table, knelt in front of Kevin and Juanita and took Kevin's left hand into her right hand and Juanita's right hand into her left hand and squeezed them. Her brother knelt down beside her a few seconds later.

"Mom… Dad… we desperately need your help," Angel Boy said. "Our world… your future…needs saving and only the two of you can help us do it."

"But, in order to do that," Angelica said, "You must learn from the past and look to the future."

Kevin Edwards and Juanita Grayson
will return in...

S.O.L.A.D™:
"Look to the Future"

Book III of S.O.L.A.D.™:
The Angelo™ & Angeline™
Chronicles

&

Big Spain™:

The Daniel Spain™
Chronicles

Coming
Soon

Acknowledgements

First, as always, I want to thank God for the vision

He gave me of Kevin Edwards, Juanita Grayson and

their amazing story. I also thank Him for the gift of

writing He has bestowed on me and given me

responsibility for. Once again, to God be the glory, the

praise and the recognition for the story that unfolded in

the pages of this book and the stories to come in

upcoming novels in this series, because without Him,

S.O.L.A.D.™ would not exist.

Second, I want to thank my wife Tajuana, who is a

blessing from God. The strength, love and partnership

that Kevin and Juanita share are just a small glimpse of

the strength, love and partnership I share with my wife.

She's so much more than a superhero and I'm so

blessed to get to spend my life with her. Both of our fathers passed last year, seven weeks apart, and God has helped us to cleave to each other and help each other through this difficult transition. I'm so thankful to have her by my side.

Third, I want to thank my family for their love, support and strength. My mom, Marjorie, continues to encourage me as I pursue my career as an author and is also anxiously awaiting the novel of my short story, "Crystal Clear". Don't worry mom. It's coming soon. My father, Tyrone Sr., who has passed from this earthly realm and now resides in Heaven with our heavenly Father, asked about Book II of S.O.L.A.D.™ every time I spoke with him before he passed last year. I wish he could have seen it completed on this side, but I'm sure God gave him an advanced copy. I miss you so much, Dad, and I will continue to make you proud. To my sister, Tameika, thank you for being so supportive and stepping up to take care of our parents, especially when I was not able to. Your reward is in Heaven, but I know God is going to continue blessing you here on earth also. To the rest of my family and friends, thank you so much for being awesome and so loving and supportive as we mourn my father's and my wife's father's passings, celebrate their homegoing and continue to accomplish the dreams and purpose God has put us on this earth for.

Thank you to my beta readers (Mom, Tameika, Tajuana and my dear, supportive friend, Ashley Holzhausen) for always doing their best to make these novels the best. I appreciate your time, love, support, edits and suggestions and I look forward to having you all as beta readers on future projects. A special thanks to Ashley for the idea to use the S.O.L.A.D.™ ring logos as scene dividers.

I also want to thank my hometown, the city of my birth, Memphis, Tenn. I love this city and I only want the best for it. I love the people who live there and I pray for them consistently. Memphis is a great city and I pray that the people who live here will continue to strive and exceed that greatness.

To the media companies and personalities honored in this novel, please keep up the great work. I love journalism and one of my dreams has always been to be a great journalist. I know so many great journalists that I'm afraid if I began naming them off, I would skip someone. I just want to say again to them, keep up the great work and thanks for being great role models of what true journalism is.

To Jennifer Cole, congratulations on winning a contest to be featured in this novel. You're a great person and I loved meeting you and your husband Neil at Superman Celebration. For those who love all things

Superman, check out Superman Super Site (www.supermansupersite.com), which Neil is chief editor and Jennifer is co-editor of.

To Victoria, a sixth-grader at Family Christian School, thank you for loving the first book so much that you wanted to be a character in the second book. This character is going to be seen in future books and play an intricate role in the series.

Finally, I want to thank you, the reader, for sticking with me on this amazing journey of a God-given vision about a soon-to-be legendary story of love, loss, action, family, possibilities, regret, war and peace that spans across several generations (in a series of novels), "from one world to the next."

I pray you enjoyed this vision and will share it with others. God Bless.

-Tyrone Tony Reed Jr.
October 2015

About the

S.O.L.A.D.™

novel series

Find out more about the novel series by visiting the websites below:

The Official Website of Tyrone Tony Reed Jr.
www.tyronetonyreedjr.com

S.O.L.A.D™ Official Facebook Page
www.facebook.com/soladchronicles

About the Author

Inspired as a child by Superman's alter ego Clark Kent, a go-getter reporter at The Daily Planet, Tyrone Tony Reed Jr.'s writing career began in his teen years.

He was a Teen Panelist for The Commercial Appeal, in Memphis, Tenn., for two years and a reporter for The Teen Appeal newspaper, also in Memphis, for three years.

While earning his journalism degree at Franklin College in Franklin, Ind., Tyrone held several positions on the college's newspaper, The Franklin.

Tyrone also worked as a crime reporter for four years at The Jackson Sun in Jackson, TN.

He is now a freelance writer, who is working on the third and fourth novels in the **S.O.L.A.D.™: Soldiers of Light Against Darkness™** series.

Tyrone's short stories appear in the books **With Great Power** and **Main Street Publishing, Inc. Presents Enlightenment: The Talent Among Us: Volume XI (Stories and Poems by Tennessee Writers) and Main Street Publishing, Inc. Presents Awakenings: The Talent Among Us: Volume XIV (Stories and Poems by Tennessee Writers).**

Tyrone lives with his wife Tajuana and their wacky dog, Kizzie.

Tyrone can be contacted at **wearesolad@outlook.com.**

Please leave a **review** for this novel by emailing Tyrone at **wearesolad@outlook.com,** leaving a message with your review on **www.tyronetonyreedjr.com/the-contact,** leaving a review on **Amazon** at **http://amzn.to/1VTWnah** and on **Goodreads** at **http://bit.ly/21LawKx.**

If you loved this book, please share your review and your thoughts on social media (Facebook, Twitter, Instagram, etc.) THANKS!!!

How to Become a
Soldier of Light Against Darkness™

You may be going through some difficult situations or you might feel everything is going well for you.

But deep down inside, you feel something, a special something, is missing in your life. That something can't be replaced with money, drugs, sex or anything else.

That something is a relationship with Jesus Christ. You see Jesus died for all of us, just so we could have the opportunity to be saved from an eternity in Hell.

God loves us so much and that is why He sent his son Jesus to Earth, so that we could be reconciled to Him and live a life free and separated from sin.

If you have tried everything to fill the emptiness in your life and still that emptiness remains, I ask you to try a life with Jesus as your Savior.

All you have to do is believe that Jesus is the Son of God and that he died for your sins.

Ask God to forgive you for all your sins and believe that He has and you are forgiven and now saved.

Saved from what, you ask? Saved from being separated from God, our Heavenly Father. Saved from a life of sin and shame. Saved from an eternity in Hell.

There might be times that you slip up and sin, but quickly ask God for forgiveness and strength to resist that sin.

It's not easy being a Soldier of Light, but God is with you and will keep you strong, courageous and prepared to fight against darkness. Read your bible, pray and find a great church home where you can fellowship with others and grow in God.

Let your light shine and always remember, I'm praying for you!

-Tyrone Tony Reed Jr.